ONE TONGUE SINGING

Susan Mann was born in Durba[...]
She spent eleven years workin[...]
a copywriter, and now teaches [...]
Town's Film and Media Programme. She lives in Cape
Town.

Susan Mann

ONE TONGUE
SINGING

VINTAGE

Published by Vintage 2005

2 4 6 8 10 9 7 5 3 1

Copyright © Susan Mann 2004

Susan Mann has asserted her right under the Copyright, Designs and Patents Act, 1988 to be identified as the author of this work

First published in Great Britain in 2004 by
Secker & Warburg

Vintage
Random House, 20 Vauxhall Bridge Road,
London SW1V 2SA

Random House Australia (Pty) Limited
20 Alfred Street, Milsons Point, Sydney
New South Wales 2061, Australia

Random House New Zealand Limited
18 Poland Road, Glenfield,
Auckland 10, New Zealand

Random House (Pty) Limited
Endulini, 5A Jubilee Road, Parktown 2193,
South Africa

The Random House Group Limited Reg. No. 954009
www.randomhouse.co.uk/vintage

A CIP catalogue record for this book
is available from the British Library

ISBN 0 099 45912 4

Papers used by Random House are natural, recyclable products made from wood grown in sustainable forests. The manufacturing processes conform to the environmental regulations of the country of origin

Printed and bound in Great Britain by
Bookmarque Ltd, Croydon, Surrey

For Glen

Part I

We are our own demons, we expel ourselves
from our paradise.

> – Goethe

History chokes on the little bones
of meaning, the little bones
of love.

> – Anne Michaels

Part I

SHE IS RUNNING. Hair matted, dress torn and filthy, eyes swollen. Her face a mucousy mess. She pushes blindly as tangled branches cut in front of her, and thorns tear at her skin. The wind keeps coming at her like a lasso, whipping up dust into her open mouth. An animal screams. She does not stop for a second. Does not utter a sound. Her only contribution to the rustles and cries of the earth is her breath, sharp and shallow, and the crackle of her bare feet trampling over leaves, broken twigs, thorns and dung. For hours she has been running, faster and faster. Into the jaws of the mountain; into the arms of the night.

She is six years old. Just six years old.

ONE

IN THE STILL heat of a late Cape February, Jake
Coleman lies awake again. He shifts position for the
umpteenth time. No need to confirm the hour from the
art deco alarm clock pulsing steadily next to his head.
From the oppressive silence he already knows it is
somewhere around three. Suicide hour. Death by suffocation. Suffocation by silence. The night is unbearably
quiet. Crickets no longer vibrate. Beetles no longer buzz.
Only the occasional jeer of a mosquito pokes the
stillness.

With eyes that burn with wakefulness and a mind
bristling with an annoying clarity, he glances across at
his sleeping partner. Maria's ample form engulfs his
space. Monopolises the cotton sheets. Her arm slops
heavily over the edge of the bed and a thin line of saliva
trickles from the corner of her mouth onto the crumpled
cotton pillowcase.

He sighs. Maria is upset with him again. And
probably back to popping pills. One for sleeping, one
for waking, one for smiling. Enslaved by pharma-
ceuticals. He knows it was the phone-call that afternoon
that set it off. She lifted the receiver, said hello, and the
person on the other end hung up. Simple as that.

Again he sighs. If only he could explain it to her, he
thinks. If only he could just admit to her that he does not

believe in love. Or at least not in her concept of it. If only he could simply confess that in his opinion, to love only one person is a rather irritating, middle-class, female preoccupation. The meagre product of a supreme lack of imagination. The demise of a mind small enough to be hemmed in by garden fences, corporate success stories and fifteen days' leave per annum . . . And in this country, the scenario would usually come complete with razor-wire trimmings and two corpulent, gas-filled Staffordshire bull terriers. The thought snakes down his spine. No, it is not for him, definitely not for him. For a man like him to be expected to love only one woman . . . ! After all, his entire life has been devoted to the pursuit of beauty.

His entire life. His fame. His painting. *Shit!* The panic tightens his throat, pricks his palms with needles of perspiration. Once again, the same swollen thoughts swelter malevolently in his brain, choking him, destroying him. If he doesn't produce something soon, he can kiss his career goodbye. Because while he will always have the school, he knows how fickle the art world can be. It does not take long for people to forget who you are.

If only Maria would understand. He watches her sleeping. Wishes she were awake so that he could take her generous hand and hold it. She had been so comforting earlier today, before that phone-call. So assuring. Confirming that people were still paying handsomely for an original Coleman, not only locally, but in many far-off places. 'Of course you're still popular, Jake,' she had said, running her manicured nails through his hair. 'People are asking for you all the time at the gallery.' Then she had gone on to remind him about all those students passionate about painting flocking from all over the country to The Jake Coleman International School of Fine Art to learn, to absorb like cotton swabs a fragment of his genius. He wishes she would wake up, so that she could tell him again.

Because for months Jake has produced nothing. There is a disturbing fear in him that his work lacks life and purpose. His expression is two-dimensional. People may be buying because he is still fashionable. And well marketed. But if probed, nobody would really know why. Critics are silent and gallery owners know better than to amputate a sure source of income. But none of this fools the Doctor of Fine Art himself.

At least there is the school, to help take his mind off it all during the day. Although even that has lost its allure lately. His thoughts rewind back to the new students who enrolled the previous week. Predictable as ever. Always two types. The first: suburban angels. Private school products. Apple of Mummy and Daddy's fond gaze. Affluently dressed with teeth individually arranged by good orthodontists. Their faces flat and shiny. Flat with inexperience. And shiny with idealism and expectation. Too young to know it is the experience of life that creates art. Too cosseted to understand it is our dark side, with its memories, its secrets and its shadows, that ultimately defines us.

Then there is the other kind: dirty, hung-over and profoundly talented in a haphazard, disorientated kind of way. The kind who stagger bleary-eyed into the first lecture like misplaced vagrants. Still smelling of last night's excesses, heavy-lidded and queasy. The kind who are never 100 per cent certain that the tattered T-shirt or vest thrown carelessly over their junk-food-filled bodies in a vague attempt at respectability, belongs to them. Nor care. The kind who look as though they brought their tattoos, pierced nostrils and tongues with them from the womb.

But they are always there. The paragons and the pariahs. For a second this affirmation is like warm milk to a fractious child. He is brilliant. Special. Not one person from the hand-picked group ever misses a class. Not a Coleman class. And no matter which bed they crawl out of each morning, he can pick up the scent of their adoration like a hungry bloodhound.

Of course, a school of fine art as prestigious as his will always attract some weirdos. Take today for example. He had only just finished his last class, sat down in his office, when there was a knock at the door. Thinking it was a student, he called 'Come in.' He had no idea it would be a complete stranger. (And how he'd found his way past Trudy at reception he has still not worked out.) The man looked like a cross between a Jesus freak and some ancient European relic. A navy beret covered some of his thick white hair. He had a long white beard and weatherbeaten skin. Jack sat back in his chair and blinked as this character, in his old worn trousers, rough cream shirt and leather sandals, opened the door, and then pushed it open further with a gnarled, wooden walking stick.

'Can I help you?' he enquired. The old man stared at him with bright blue eyes for quite some time, before answering 'Yes'. His voice was thin and raspy and foreign. Then very slowly he sat down. Equally slowly, he asked how his granddaughter could enrol at the school. Jake was well-accustomed to dealing with parents who held inflated opinions of their child's talents. They drove expensive cars, wore expensive jewellery and bought their children expensive educations. They were nothing like this man, who looked as though he had just flown in on some hessian carpet.

'I'm afraid the school is already full this year, and most likely for next too. She will have to apply next year.'

'Just have a look at her work before you decide,' the old man said.

'I'm afraid we're already oversubscribed, with a long waiting list as it is. She will have to bring me her portfolio, and then if she complies with the regulations and has sufficient talent, she can go on next year's waiting list.'

Whether the old foreigner understood him or not, or whether he was just being stubborn, Jake still can't work out.

'Tomorrow then.' He leaned heavily on his stick, rising. His hands knotted with history, like the branches of an oak. In his smoky voice, he repeated, 'Tomorrow. She will be here tomorrow.'

He started to explain that tomorrow would be impossible, with classes all day, but the old man simply tipped his beret and left.

As he lies here now it suddenly strikes him that he should have told the visitor what the fees were. Silly old git probably has no idea what tertiary education fees run at in 2001. There were other places she could go. The Jake Coleman International School of Fine Art is aimed at a niche market. He should have explained that.

He glares at the clock with gritty eyes. Its green hands, glowing in the dark like malevolent teeth, point to a quarter to four. The silence cramps. Adrenalin thumps. And night is a fist banging like a lunatic at some abandoned door.

He is still awake when the first bird begins its morning chant. In the distance the rough palpitation of the day's first train. He watches Maria draining the dregs of sleep from the night, before slowly stirring. Sees her stumble sleepily to the bathroom. Hears the bath running, the toilet flushing, cupboards opening, no doubt to find her latest range of aromatherapy bath salts. A while later she reappears. He peers at her through heavy lids as she marches towards the mirror, swaddled in bathgown, a tiny mascara wand in her large, jewelled hand. Watches her assess the well-coiffed hair from one side, then the other, as it glints expensively in the morning light. With her right hand she ruffles it just the slightest bit, so that it looks natural. Then leans forward and pulls her lips over her teeth to scrape away some overgenerous lipstick from her mouth, before blotting it with a tissue. The mouth he once found sexy, full of humour. She seems withdrawn. Almost unaware of him. She rises from the dressing table with a sigh, lets the luxurious bathrobe fall to the floor and digs in her underwear drawer. How sturdy she is. And how buxom and high her breasts after the little operation she had last year. If he weren't so tired he would definitely try to entice her back to bed. He remembers a time when exquisite French underwear such as that would have lasted all of three seconds on her, before he whipped it off. She picks out a dress in peach Irish linen. Natural fabric of course.

'Morning,' he offers.

'Morning,' she clips, walking back to the dressing table.

'Off so quickly this morning?'

'I have a meeting first thing at the gallery with that foreigner.' She squints while removing with a little brush any errant clumps of mascara from the rather coarse lashes.

She is talking. A good sign. He smiles.

'Is that the Hungarian you've been speaking about?'

'Yes, Mátyás is his name. I haven't met him yet. But Cecily tells me his pottery is really something. This is the second time I've arranged to meet him. The first time he didn't pitch up. Silly man, doesn't realise how much publicity I could get him. Honestly, I don't know how half these people eat.'

'I feel awful,' he says in a small voice. 'Didn't sleep again.'

'You should get up, Jake, you'll be late.'

She has not forgotten.

He grunts. Normally she would have brought him tea if she were up first. In fact, it is unusual for Maria to be up this early. For her, a meeting 'first thing' usually means a cup of steaming Turkish coffee in an avant-garde mug with a colleague or aspiring artist at the avant-garde coffee shop next to her avant-garde art gallery in Constantia. Sitting among the likes of those who have either just booked their annual skiing holiday or bought first-class plane tickets to Cannes from the travel agency close by.

'Lunch?' he suggests sweetly. That should do it. Maria is such a pushover when it comes to food.

'Call me,' she says, grabbing her gym bag, and walking through the door, trailing a haze of Calvin Klein's *Obsession* like a jet stream behind her.

She has not kissed him goodbye.

TWO

IT IS ONE of those forgotten little patches of earth. An overgrown hedge hides the overgrown garden. A few painted stones lead to a tiny cottage, no more than a tin-roof rondavel. Red tin, freshly painted. If you were to walk up this gravel pathway, hedged with French lavender, to its thick, whitewashed walls and peer through the window, you would see a small room: a worn rug on the wooden slatted floor. A newspaper, open, on a table covered in crisp, blue-checked cloth. Three battered leather chairs on wooden bases, a mohair blanket folded on one of them. A lamp with a red shade perched on the shelf above the fireplace. An old gas stove and sink in the far corner. The walls are covered with a child's drawings, backed and framed with cardboard stuck on with sticky tape. Two doors, both open, lead into two little nooks, each with a wooden bed, white covers, a piece of mirror on the wall, and more drawings.

Zara has woken early. Slips out carefully from under the sheet so as not to wake Maman. Laika, the Labrador-cross pup, follows her into the living room, and lies alongside her where she sprawls on the rug. Pappi, her grandfather, has given her a new colouring book and a new box of wax crayons with a sharpener. A present from the horses, he said. She has coloured every page already, and is going back to add more detail when she hears the rustle of leaves outside. Ah, she thinks. She has been expecting this. She climbs up on the chair, pulls the muslin curtain aside and looks out of the window. Something is moving in the hedge. She *knew* it . . . She tiptoes over the wooden floors to the door, reaches up on her toes and strains to undo the latch. Too heavy. She tiptoes back across the slats, and returns carrying some books, which she stacks one on top of the other. She steps up onto the books and with brow furrowed and arms straining, finally manages to turn the key. She opens the door very slowly, stops to make sure she can still hear Pappi snoring in his room, then steps barefoot out onto the stoep.

Even though the sun is barely up, it is hot. She pulls her nightdress over her head and drops it on the step. Stands naked, peering at the hedge. No movement. She feels the wet muzzle of the dog against the back of her leg. 'Shhhhh, Laika . . .' The two of them tread gingerly across the uneven, coarse grass, past the oak tree with the swing, towards the hedge. Zara parts the branches, and finds herself face to face with a little brown girl, even smaller than herself. The two stare at one another, wide-eyed, without smiling. Eventually, Zara leans forward, raises a very straight eyebrow and whispers, 'I knew you'd come. Are you a fairy?'

The brown girl stares back. 'Wat?'

'Are you a fairy?'

The brown girl does not blink. She has heard English before. Repeats what she knows.

'Issa Hotnot.'

'Is that a kind of fairy?'

Unsure of the question, she says the second thing she knows in English. 'My name is Blom September.'

Then, at a loss at what to do next, and as a token of solidarity, she whips off her little dress too.

A little later, Camille wakes at the sound of a dog barking. She pats the bed, calls out for her daughter in her low sleepy voice 'Zara . . .? Laika . . .?' When she receives no response, she sits up and stretches to look out the window, pushing a tangle of dark curls away from her face. She sees a brown child and a white child, both naked, playing on the swing. The higher they go, with their legs straight out, the louder the dog barks.

Blom is back again the next day. And the day after. Camille tries to find out where she comes from, but the child speaks Afrikaans and does not understand English very well. At first all questions are met either with 'Issa Hotnot', or 'My name is Blom September', the latter uttered with utmost seriousness and imperious authority.

The language of play seems unconfined by words. Both children chatter on in their own tongue, nodding and pointing, whether they are drawing, climbing the oak tree or playing on the swing. Unsurprisingly, Blom is the more insistent communicator of the two, often taking Zara's hand and repeating herself over and again until she is certain Zara has understood her. Camille cannot help being a little relieved that Zara finally has a playmate; particularly one that seems to bring her out of her shell. Things have not been easy since they arrived in the valley a few years ago. Especially with Zara being such an unusual, serious child.

Very soon the children play daily. Blom is picking up English very quickly, and Zara some Afrikaans. This, added to the French she knows from listening to her mother and grandfather, is making for some very interesting combinations. While Camille has made a considerable effort to speak English to Zara in this non-French-speaking country, she cannot help noticing that it is not the language her child elects to use when she needs some colour. Camille may be unfamiliar with Afrikaans herself, but knows her usually contained child well enough to pick up the emotional nuances of '*Quelle horreur! Jou bliksem*', when Blom breaks one of her crayons. Grandpapa is no longer only 'Pappi', but 'Oupappi' too. And only last week, after supper, when Zara spilt chocolate milk all over a drawing, Camille overheard her mutter 'Oh fok' under her breath.

And then one morning everything changes. Camille, Zara and her grandfather are about to have breakfast, when Laika starts barking, as though to herald the start of what sounds like a terrible commotion outside. They run to the window to see Blom being beaten by a woman. Blom is screaming while the older woman shouts, '*Ek het jou hoeveel keer gesê . . . jy moenie by wit mense gaan nie . . . wil jy hê dat ons van die farm weggegooi word? Huh? Wil jy? Wil jy?*'

Camille runs down the steps, the old man close behind her. The older woman looks up, holds off another blow with an explanation.

'Askies, Merrem, I'm sorrie about this chile of mine. I told her before not to go wondering all fancy-like into white people's houses. But you think she listens? Nee wat. She got her own fancy ideas. She says she's going to play by the dam, and today, I follow her, jus to make sure, and then I see her coming here. She won't come here again, I promise you. Jus, please don't tell Meneer. It won't happen again. I promise. I'm sorrie, Merrem.'

'Wait . . .' Camille walks right up to her. 'I don't understand. Are you Blom's mother?'

'Ja, Merrem.'

'What is your name?'

'Leah September, Merrem.'

'I'm Camille. Camille Pascal. Who don't you want me to tell?' She holds out her hand. Leah looks embarrassed and pretends not to notice.

She knows exactly who Camille Pascal is. She doesn't have to be told. Since she arrived in the valley a few years ago, all fancy-like in her bright dresses and high heels and lots of hair, everybody is talking. The men, blerrie fools, act blind and dumb, of course. But the women – even Mevrou Smit – they know trouble when they see it.

'Who don't you want me to tell?' Camille repeats.

'Isn't yous not part of Meneer Smit's farm, Merrem?'

'Absolutely not! No, this little piece of land and the cottage are ours. We bought it from Meneer Smit five years ago when we came from France. We have nothing to do with Meneer Smit, or his wine farm.'

'Oh.' The relief falls like light over her face. 'My husband and I is working for Meneer Smit. My husband onna farm, you know, with the grapes. Me inna house. But Meneer doesn't like it when the kinders come up to the house. He doesn't like it. And things is tough enough as it is . . .' Her voice trails off. 'Anyways, I thought yous was somehow part of Meneer Smit's . . . I dunno . . .'

Leah can still remember the way everybody talked when the cottage was suddenly occupied. Nobody even knew it was for sale – they used to say it mus' be haunted – and then next thing this old car drives up to the big house, and this young women she comes inna house in this big skirt, tight top, big hair and asks if she can buy it. And Meneer Smit, the *poephol*, is all smiling with his yellow teeth and sticking his chest out like a

16

kalkoen, saying he is sure it can be arranged, and Mevrou Smit is later saying it is shameless how he behaved. And nobody knows if it was bought or what is the story.

'Anyways,' she continues, 'my chile mustn't bother you again anyways.'

'She's no bother, Mrs September. We're very fond of Blom. She's welcome here any time. Please, come inside, would you like some coffee?'

Leah September actually jumps.

'*Nie, dankie, ek kannie.* I mus go back to the big house.'

But Blom September is allowed to stay and play.

THREE

'AND THEN OF course, painting is also process,' he explains to the class. 'A bridge across the chasm of our unknowing. It is about creating our own meaning. To use the old cliché, it is a journey. Our interpretation of the journey. And our paintbrushes are the little integrators, finding some balance between light and shadow, the synthesis of ideas, or of all the disparate elements in a single moment. There is a rather lovely image for this; the poet Rilke likens artistic balance to a "folding of hands". Through medium and colour we create the texture, the flavour of an emotion. And there are often surprises on the way. Little truths that you never even knew, that find their way onto the canvas.'

It is a small class. They do not know each other well yet. And although their quest for individual expression makes them unlikely ever to become a team, he usually finds that a comfortable cohesion develops as the year progresses. He watches a girl with a strappy sundress lean over to pick up her pencil. The strap falls away from the roundness of her shoulder onto her suntanned arm. She does not bother to adjust it. Looks up at him with bright green eyes. Just behind her, another girl with short blonde curls and enormous breasts leans back, puts her arms behind her head. A libidinous bunch, he reckons. As if reading his mind, a boy with sleepy eyes raises his hand.

'Yes?'

'Painting is also desire.'

'I don't know about painting *being* desire. It can certainly be an expression of desire. Depending on our definition of desire. It can capture a facet, a moment, the urge that moves us from ourselves towards the other. And it can be extremely intimate. The relationship between a painter and his work . . .'

'But what can be more intimate than desire?' the sleepy boy interrupts.

'Fulfilling desire may be intimate. But intimacy and desire are not always bedfellows, so to speak. In fact, I'm sure you can all think of many examples of intimacy that do not necessarily include desire. And if any of you have had a one-night stand, you'll already know that desire need not include intimacy.'

He enjoys debating these issues with his students. It adds dimension to their work. And it breaks the ice on a day like today, when the year is still new.

'Let's throw it open to the floor,' he suggests. 'Think of some examples of intimacy that do not include the obvious.'

The boy lowers his heavy lids in contemplation. The rest of the class follow Jake with their eyes.

'Intimacy is the smell of a slept-in T-shirt,' the girl with the breasts offers.

'It's having a really honest conversation,' says another.

'It's the first light of morning on a sleeping person's face.'

'It's his hands, curled like a child, while sleeping.'

'I suppose the idea of slippers in the cupboard is still getting bad press?'

The class laughs.

'Or maybe it's just acceptance,' says the girl with the strappy dress.

'Yes, tolerance! It's the new South Africa,' someone sniggers.

A good time to end the lecture.

'This may be a good subject for our next painting assignment. The good thing about asking questions like these, is that for each of us, the answer may be different. Which means each of us has a unique opportunity to express our own individual truth, to offer others a piece of ourselves, and sometimes themselves too.'

As he leaves the lecture room, he shakes his head. All this head knowledge and still no answers for himself. Perhaps it is simply a matter of finding the right question . . . He rubs his eyes. If only he could just get one decent night's sleep! He passes the secretary's office, runs an appreciative glance over Trudy, standing at the filing cabinet in a knee-length floral dress and high-heeled sandals. Great ankles. She turns, smiles, holds his eye for a split second.

Trudy does not warn him. In fact, she does not even know that he is in for a surprise. Had she known, she may have tried to prevent it from ever happening, right there and then. Instead, she watches fondly as he continues on his way, down the passage to his office. Sees him open the door and step inside before the wind closes it with a bang behind him. Trudy has no idea that standing by the window, behind his desk, is a young woman looking out. Trudy could never imagine the amazed look on Jake's face as he gapes at the intruder. In spite of the sound of the door banging, the visitor does not turn around immediately. She simply stands there in a dark green oversized T-shirt and a long, shapeless skirt, gazing out into space. Until he says, 'Can I help you?'

Then slowly, as if in a dream, she turns and faces him.

If this had been a man he would probably have asked him to leave. And pretty curtly too. But this isn't a man. It is a woman, unkempt, young. Or maybe not, it's hard to say. Her eyes, big and black, are completely opaque. She has long hair, dark and matted, that falls to her waist. With her pale skin, hollowed-out eyes and angular features, she reminds him of a rather grubby ghost. He blinks, runs his hand through his hair and clears his throat. He can feel his cheeks growing warmer.

'Who are you and how did you get in here?' This is the second day in a row that Trudy has allowed a stranger simply to waltz into his office. He must speak to her about it.

She looks directly at him. She seems neither embarrassed nor apologetic.

'Would you like to sit down?' he tries eventually, and clears his throat again.

She moves from the window towards the chair. Sits down. In *his* seat. He stares at her in open-mouthed amazement. Then he slowly settles down in what should be her chair, perching uncomfortably on the edge of it. She meets his stare very directly, with dense ebony eyes. She neither speaks nor smiles. She hands him the folder in her hands. He finds it all very disconcerting and shifts in his seat and clears his throat, taking the folder from her as a welcome escape from her gaze. It is not that she is staring *at* him. He would be fairly comfortable with that; it is the fact that she appears to be looking straight *through* him, as though he did not exist.

Suddenly a thought strikes him. 'Are you perhaps related to the elderly gentleman who came to see me yesterday?'

She gives something between a nod and a shrug.

He really should send her away right now. There is no space for another student. It's not as though he didn't say all that yesterday to the old man.

And then he opens the folder.

In years to come this will remain one of the most significant points in his memory. The moment he first saw the paintings of Zara Pascal. They do not show any particular excellence of style; in truth her style is inconsistent and difficult to fathom. But the sheer impact of the subject, the total lack of indecision when it comes to colour, the raw intensity of her pieces are so powerful that they bypass the critical faculties, penetrating something dark within like a flaming arrow. Each painting is of a wild animal in savage attack. In each painting an animal has been killed or is doing the killing. It is as though she has painted the first convulsive shock of death from the inside, the movement of the musculature, the gleam of blood and teeth and claws, the raging mix of elation and terror in their eyes. In each case it is the precision of that death moment, captured in yellow-reds and violet-purples, that creates such a terrifying impact. He would never forget a single one of them.

This time he looks up at her, really looks. But he cannot make the connection. The relationship between this expressionless young woman and the raw violence of her art is quite beyond him.

Words fall from his mouth before he can change his mind. As though something else is speaking through him.

'Would you come back tomorrow?' he says. 'We start classes at nine.'

Immediately after he has said this, he shakes his head. He should be sending her away. How can he just back down like that? But then she may never return; and frankly that is not a risk he is prepared to take.

'And would you leave your portfolio with me? I'd like to take a proper look when I have time.'

Her face remains blank. Then, as simply as she had sat down, she gets up and walks out of the door empty-handed, without uttering a word.

Later that night, once Maria has fallen asleep, he gets up and opens her portfolio again. Extraordinary. Alarming, really, considering her age. He sits for a long time in the lounge. Maria's book, *The Dalai Lama Pocketbook,* lies open on the coffee table next to the couch where she had been chatting on the phone. Underneath it, between some travel brochures, lies another book she has recently bought, *Abundance: A Lifestyle You Deserve*. Beneath that, his battered version of Nietzsche's *Thus Spake Zarathustra*. Zara. Thustra. He pulled it out only last week. Funny how things like that happen. The name on the young woman's portfolio is Zara Pascal.

He pops a CD of Mozart's *Don Giovanni* into the player, returns to the sofa thinking how strange she was. Takes another look at her paintings. He has not been able to get them out of his mind. Their violence lingers on the psyche; he can almost smell the warm, sweet pungency of blood. Who is she? And why does he find her so disturbing? Is it because he cannot find a category for her? Doesn't know how to label her? Her face is still very young – she cannot be more than twenty. But her eyes are not the eyes of a young woman. There is nothing of the innocence of youth in them. No naivety. They tell you nothing; give nothing away.

FOUR

BEHIND THE COTTAGE, beyond the vines, the two children have discovered the vague hint of a path. They already know that if you follow it carefully a short way, it will take you over the coarse mountain grass, till you reach a clear, shallow pool of water; the base of a small waterfall. This haven for rock rabbits, tadpoles and the occasional wildcat, hidden among trees and boulders, has become their secret; close enough to the cottage for them to hear Camille calling, yet far enough from things too ordinary for the serious business of make-believe.

Now that several months of playing have elapsed, and Blom has finally grasped her friend's expectations of her as a fairy, she is determined to live up to them. The two spend considerable time pivoting on rocks, flapping their arms while Blom shouts flying commands with the vigour of a sergeant major. At the sound of Laika's enthusiastic barking, Camille often walks up to check on them, treading cautiously to ensure she is never seen.

'She's teaching me to fly,' she tells Camille that night. 'She's a fairy, you know.'

'I know,' says Camille. 'I can see that. Did you hear that, Papa? Zara is having flying lessons. With a real fairy.'

'*Merveilleux*,' says Pappi absent-mindedly, reading the newspaper. 'Only wings evade death. Neruda says so.' As he turns the page he looks at Zara and makes his bright blue eyes big. 'And Neruda knows.' He reaches for his pipe.

Zara stares at him for some time. 'Was he a friend of God?'

'Who? Neruda?'

'Yes.'

'He may have been, I'm not sure, *petite*. For all we know he may even have been God.'

Or they play with mud. This involves gathering up wet, oozing river sand and smearing it all over their tiny bodies, delighting at the pinkness of their mouths, the sudden white contrast of their eyes and the uniformity of their colour.

'Now we're the same,' says Blom. 'Brown like mud.'

'Hotnots,' says Zara.

They are terribly proud of their secret hideout. Blom is already making extravagant plans to live there permanently.

'You can come and live here too, *as jy wil*,' she suggests.

'And Laika and Maman and Papa'tjie too?'

'No. No grown-ups.'

Zara cannot imagine climbing into a bed at night that does not have her mother in it.

'Fairies have mothers,' she ventures. 'They do.'

'Issie. No mothers en no fathers. Jus' other fairies.'

'Just other fairies?' Zara is surprised. For the first time she starts to feel sorry for them.

'Well, not the Hotnot kind, anyways,' says Blom confidently.

'We could invite them here, for a party,' she says, hoping to change Blom's mind.

'No. No grown-ups.' Blom is firm. 'Unless . . .'

'What?'

'Unless, we make a concert.'

'A concert?'

'Ja. A concert. Fairies is verrie good at concerts. Singing en dancing.'

'And flying,' adds Zara.

'Ja, en flying,' agrees Blom optimistically. 'We can stan' op daai rock,' she says, pointing to one of the favoured flying pedestals. 'En they can sit oppie gras.'

And so rehearsals begin.

They have no idea that all this time they are being watched. The brown eyes of a small boy with short spiky hair follow their every movement. He has a number of hiding places: the enormous tree with convoluted branches that spreads its leafy carapace over the pool, the murky, moss-filled cave behind the waterfall; and in the little troughs between the huge granite boulders. He does not dare speak to them. He cannot understand what they are saying half the time, anyway. He simply waits and watches, blinking into the dappled light, every day.

He hears Zara teach Blom 'Au Clair de la Lune'. Over and over she repeats each line, with Blom stopping and starting and repeating, her voice rising clear and uninhibited into the sky. He watches Blom teach Zara to 'jive', swaying her hips, all the while singing and clicking her small fingers, for rhythm. The two are trying to keep in time; a struggle with Blom forever inventing new steps and losing the sequence.

At the end of the day, he follows them back to the cottage, before making his own way home. He keeps a distance behind them, stopping and waiting, ducking behind rocks and bushes. And then they disappear behind the stable door. Sometimes a pretty lady with long, dark hair comes out to meet them and hoses them down, both squealing and squirming, to get rid of the mud. Often an old man sits on the stoep smoking a pipe, writing something with a pencil in the newspaper. Then usually a little later the brown girl reappears, closing the door behind her with a bang before slipping into the late-afternoon shadows.

He longs to know what happens inside the cottage; what they talk about, what they eat. Even after he has been put to bed at night, he imagines them sitting in that very small house, and wishes he could be there too. Had he been able to see Zara right then, he would be intrigued: she is on the floor with her crayons, creating a poster for the concert and making invitations. There are to be five invitees: Maman, Pappi, Laika, and Blom's parents, Goiya and Leah September. The poster is a drawing of a white girl, a brown girl and a dog – all with wings.

And then he almost ruins it all. A few weeks after the start of the concert preparations, rehearsals are interrupted by the appearance of a mongoose. The girls stalk it quietly and slowly. The boy readjusts himself on the branch so that he can keep them in view. And suddenly, without so much as a warning wobble, he loses his balance. With a thud he falls out of the tree. The two girls stop in their tracks, their eyes wide. They are unsure whether to be frightened or impressed.

'*Jissslaaik!*' says Blom.

He jumps to his feet, dusts the dirt from his khaki shorts.

'*En nou? Wie die fok is jy?*' enquires Blom, her head at an angle, her tiny hands on her hips.

The boy blinks.

27

'Was die matter? Don't you *parle die taal*?' she continues, glancing at Zara knowingly.

He does not understand a word. But he can tell by her clenched fingers and burning glare that the spritely brown girl is angry with him. He feels desperate. What a mistake to make! Now they will always check to see whether he is there.

'So, boy, as jy kannie talk, kan jy sing?' demands Blom.

At last, a sentence he thinks he understands. And an opportunity to redeem himself.

'Sing?'

'Ja, sing!'

So deep is his longing to be accepted by the two, so strong his admiration for them, that, in the smallest voice, focusing on a yellow beetle on the ground, he starts to sing the song he has learned best by watching and listening:

> *Au clair de la lune*
> *Mon ami Pierrot*
> *Prête-moi ta plume*
> *Pour écrire un mot.*'

When he has finished, he looks up, the awkward glow of embarrassment still burning in his cheeks. Blom is about to reprimand him when she is interrupted.

'That's very good,' says Zara. And then, to her friend's indignation and disgust, she walks over to where he is standing awkwardly and puts a muddy hand in his. 'What's your name?'

Many years from now when he thinks back to these first secret months and that first moment when he replied 'Pieter', in a soft whisper, he will recognise that even then he hadn't known what to say to her, or who to be. Even then he had felt clumsy and uncouth in her world. Her other world.

The day of the concert brings the first rains of autumn. With renewed vigour and braced by howling winds, drops like glassy needles pound an earth exhausted by summer. Dust dissolves into little rivulets and pools. And all over the valley, in the rain-softened air, the fragrance of newly soaked soil is a welcome reminder that this year's heat is finally over.

Zara is not impressed. She sits glaring out the window, with the rain pelting down on to the tin roof and dripping into a bucket in the corner of the room. Why did it have to rain today, just when they were due to give their concert this afternoon to both families? She sees an inky figure darting first between the bushes, then along the pathway, holding a plastic bag over her head. Blom.

Camille opens the door.

'What are we going to do?' Zara asks the sodden figure.

On cue, Blom bursts into tears.

'Come, *petite*, take off your wet clothes,' says Camille, motioning the old man to bring the blanket from the chair. 'Now what are all these tears about?' she asks, wrapping the worn blanket around the shivering child. 'Why don't we have the concert tomorrow?'

'What if it rains again?' Zara interjects.

'Well, if it rains tomorrow, we can have the concert here. Tomorrow is Sunday, it's still the weekend. Blom, your mother and father, they will be able to come?'

Blom remains silent, except for the occasional sniff.

'Why don't we spend the day making new invitations?

On the back, I'll write a letter to your mother asking her and your father to come over.'

No response. How could they know, Camille and her father, that the little girl had tossed the previous invitation into the bushes? The old man repeats the suggestion in his deep, thick-accented voice, as Camille goes to find a tissue for Blom to blow her nose.

'Come, Blom, we light a fire, yes?' he says.

'Yes!' says Zara. 'Blom and me will put the wood. Will you help me, Blom?'

'Awraait,' comes the despondent reply.

As she kneels down in front of the fireplace, the blanket falls from her tiny shoulders. From across the room both Camille and her father cannot fail to notice a large bruise and stripes of congealed blood across her back.

From Saturday, at one o'clock in the afternoon, till six o'clock on Monday morning, Leah September is off work. Occasionally, when Meneer and the Missus have a party on Saturday night, she is asked to come in the next day to mop up the spilt wine and snacks, clear the tables, and wash, dry and put away an endless array of wine glasses and food-encrusted plates. Sometimes, if they have change on them and are feeling generous, they give her a few rand. But mostly the aftermath of the parties leaves them hung-over and irritable, giving her the impression that they resent the fact that she is there at all. Luckily, there have been no parties this weekend. Like most Saturdays, she tells the children to go and play somewhere else, and uses her free afternoon to clean her own home.

The Septembers' home is the last in a string of six one-roomed cottages, separated by walls. The white paint is peeling from the façade, and a little way in front of their doors a wire suspended along the length of the cottages is used as a washing line. Outside, on weekends, the men sit on large upturned cans, smoking, drinking and playing dominoes, while children play naked in the sand. When it rains the men take their 4.5-litre bottle of Oom Tas and pick whichever cottage has a table. The children, bored and frustrated, run in and out in the wet.

It is dark by the time she has finished dusting, wiping, washing clothes and scrubbing the floor and is arranging the few wet garments over the basin to dry. She can hear the men shouting and arguing next door. Any minute now someone will pick a fight. Probably Goiya. She only hopes he passes out as soon as he comes back home. She picks up the bag of dust and dirt to place it outside the door. In the distance she sees two people walking towards her. She squints to see whether she can make out who it is. A small child and an old man, under an umbrella. Blom. This child of hers has been trouble from the start, she thinks. What can it be this time?

'Ja?' She is tired. Demoralised. It is dark, but she does not light a candle.

'I bring Blom home,' he says. 'We have a letter for you.'

'Hey?' she asks, struggling to understand his accent. 'Come again?'

He hands her the letter, then tips his beret and leaves.

She lights a candle before opening the letter and pulling out the single page. On the one side is a child's drawing. On the back a few lines neatly written:

Dear Leah,
    We invite you and your husband to come

tomorrow afternoon. The children will show us their concert. It will be good to see you again.

Yours,

Camille

PS I mixed some cream for Blom's back. Maybe you can help her with that.

She sighs, and sits down heavily on the mattress. That's all she needs. White people now trying to play God. She doesn't trust them one bit.

'Mine your own blerrie business,' she says under her breath. Then hoists herself up, and holding the candle to her face, looks in the piece of mirror she has stuck to the wall. Her right eye is swollen shut.

She turns to Blom and with a bitter, exaggerated English accent asks, 'Ja? And what do you suppose we do about *this* tomorrow, hey?'

FIVE

HE STANDS BEFORE the bathroom mirror, a maroon towel tucked tightly around his thickening waist, his shoulder-length sand-coloured hair still wet from the shower. He dries it off with a hand towel, and leans forward towards the mirror. He suspects his hairline is receding a little further. He lifts it in sections to check for signs of grey, wondering whether the few strands he has already noticed lend him a distinguished air, or whether they make him look seedy. With concentration, he examines his face first from one side, then the other: fair skin and round pale eyes accentuated by dark half-moons beneath them. A very straight nose, with a small dent at the top where his glasses sit. He shaves with intent; his beard has always been too patchy for the unshaven look. Then brushes his teeth and tests his smile (he has always considered that his 'feature'). After drying his hair with Maria's turbo hairdryer, he ties it back. Then stretches up as tall as his five feet seven inches will allow, breathing in, to observe with interest what he may look like were his girth not quite so generous. He holds this pose for a while, before releasing his breath and watching his middle expand once more.

He switches on his cellphone. While looking out at a grey, blustery day, he retrieves two messages, each a reminder: one from Trudy about their lunch date that afternoon, the second from Maria about a dinner engagement with the Bryants that evening. He steps into black linen pants and soft Italian leather shoes, stretches a polo-neck black T-shirt over his head, grabs the black linen jacket and Armani sunglasses, takes one final look in the mirror, then leaves.

Negotiating the traffic en route to Stellenbosch, and the school, he considers the day ahead. The Bryants: Roland Bryant is a successful business tycoon who has inherited money. With his round, rosy cheeks and unruly hair, he effuses a kind of babyish bonhomie that comes with never having suffered a day's worry in his life. There is nothing money has not bought him: status, friends, security and entertainment. He is both animated and laminated by wealth. His wife, the manicured and sleek Cecily Charlston-Bryant does not work and, as far as he knows, has no education. She did, however, attend a finishing school in Switzerland, which has equipped her with an overenunciated elocution and a passion for French champagne and travel. 'Wouldn't you simply *die* without Siena?' she says, rolling her eyes and tipping the remainder of her Laurent Perrier from the fluted glass into her pouty little mouth. She reminds him of a Pekinese. He half expects that one day one of these emphatic statements will be punctuated with an eye popping out.

But the couple own several of his paintings, which they hang all over their marble-floored Camps Bay home. And they seem to treasure having a celebrated artist to garnish their dinner table. Maria is so good that way. Networking is possibly what she does best.

Maria. What has happened to the generous, sensual woman he first met ten years ago? Nothing? Is that the

34

problem? Perhaps her consistency, her predictable adoration and perpetual forgiveness have become boring. As though through sheer excess (exactly the generosity he first found appealing) the senses have been numbed. Where does it go to, the love, when it has died?

Maria. Suspicious of his every move. Silently suffering. Struggling to 'make it work', whatever that means. She has taken to trying to surprise him in bed, confessing coyly that she read in *Cosmopolitan* that sex becomes more interesting when you do something that makes you blush when you remember it the following morning.

That is the thing about Maria: she does everything by the book. And yet he cannot deny that ten years ago meeting Maria was the turning point of his life. She was thirty-five – a year younger than himself – with a love of life like a force of nature. At that time – he was only recently divorced – it seemed to him that she really knew how to *live*. With relish. With indulgence and abandon. And a sensual urgency that rippled into everything. And she could afford to do so. Her business was import/export. Curios, artefacts, South African art. She left on planes on Mondays and returned on Fridays with deals and restaurant slips and foreign shoes and pieces of fabric for cushions. She was extravagant and generous and as passionate about him as all the other things she enjoyed.

Before he met her he had been scraping a living together, giving art classes, selling pieces during the season. But it was Maria, larger than life and fabulously wealthy, who had truly held the mirror up to his talent. Her response to his work was unabashedly sexual. She moved and sighed and caught her breath and held his arm. Sometimes she even had tears in her eyes. She established a name for him in parts of America, Holland and the Riviera, playing buyers in one country off against the others, hiking his prices up 500 per cent so that people were forced to stop and look.

The school too was her idea; initially a marketing ploy, particularly the name. The *Jake Coleman International School of Fine Art* gave it immediate prestige, which they instantly ratified by awarding a few scholarships to foreign students with talent. The timing was perfect; they were able to jump on the bandwagon of the supposedly newly liberated South Africa, and the brand kept growing. Luckily he has always loved teaching. And the students seem to feel it and thrive.

He does not mind the drive to the school, from Constantia to Stellenbosch. A chance to gather his thoughts. Even today in this howling gale. He decelerates his white BMW to accommodate traffic on De Waal Drive, glancing up at Newlands Forest; the branches of the trees Zulu dancing in the ululating wind. Digs around in the glove compartment for a CD and slips it into the player. The cool voice of Sade. After that, the highway, past cooling towers and shacks, then the landscape opens up into the soft fields and sapphire dams of the winelands, all the way into the university town of Stellenbosch.

Half an hour later, the car purrs up a bricked driveway, lined with white roses and a few tall lamps. The school is a large double-storey Cape Dutch house, thatched, with two white gables, newly varnished teak shutters and a gleaming red stone stoep. From the upper balcony, pots of bright geraniums spill over and through the railings.

The class is quieter than usual when he walks in out

of the wind. A couple of students here and there are talking in low voices. But he can sense something. Resistance? Apprehension? It is as though the air has been pulled taut. He stands at the table in the front of the classroom for a moment and casts his eye over the group, trying to work it out. And then he sees her sitting in the back row, alone. She has come back then, the strange one. She stares straight ahead, her black eyes hardly blinking. Her face is as lifeless as it was the day before and she is wearing the same bottle-green T-shirt and shapeless skirt. Her hair drops in a matted tangle onto her shoulders.

At the end of the lecture he watches the class separate and re-form, coagulating into little clots, before disappearing down the corridor. Zara waits for them all to leave before she stands.

'Did you manage to sort everything out with the secretary about your late registration?' he asks.

She nods, drops her head and hurriedly makes her way to the door.

'Welcome to the class,' he calls out. But she is already shutting the door behind her.

He has always had a fascination for uncontrived eccentricity. It is a little like uncontrived sensuality: raw and authentic. Something in him feels strangely flattered that someone like her would elect to attend his lectures, his school. The class will have to get used to her, that's all; she has clearly altered the equilibrium.

And then an incident. The first he hears of it is in an e-mail from a parent. The mother of the girl with big breasts complains that the school is unhygienic, and that she is not forking out astronomically high fees for her child to attend a cockroach-infested haven. Nonplussed, he calls the girl in and asks her to explain. It appears that the class had been waiting for him one morning, when they noticed a cockroach running across the floor. The girls lifted their feet. One of the boys jumped up to kill it. Zara pushed him away. When the boy asked her what she was doing, she replied, 'It's cleaner than you.' The boy sat down again, and a few minutes later Zara reached into her bag and threw down a bit of crust for the cockroach.

'She *fed* the cockroach?' he says.

'Yes.'

'I see.'

There is something about the girl's shocked earnestness, her sense of *outrage* – he can imagine the dinnertime conversation – that strikes him as rather hilarious. He stifles his amusement.

'Thank you. That will be all.' He cannot resist one last, fleeting glance at her chest.

In time, the class forget about the incident, and do, in fact, get used to her. Some continue to avoid speaking to her at all, or even sitting anywhere near her, as though repelled. She acts as if none of them exists. She ignores them all – even those who watch her with something akin to morbid fascination. Sometimes he notices her lips moving, as though she is talking to herself. Or commenting on something. But mostly she remains silent. What he cannot help noticing is that each and every one of them, whether through active avoidance or secret observance, is acutely aware of her presence at all times. Especially when she paints.

There is something hypnotic about her when she paints. He finds himself watching so intently that he has to jerk himself back to reality. It is as though the paintbrush becomes a little magic wand, enabling her to transcend her own blankness. As though, by holding it, she learns the secret password into another world to which she alone has access. There is a rhythm in her movement and a relaxed absorption in her subject that creates a seamlessness between the two. A symbiotic relationship.

And then there are the paintings themselves. This is becoming more and more of an enigma. She seems completely unpredictable in her interpretation of her subject. If it is a still life, she renders a quick sketch, before taking another sheet of paper and drawing something completely different; usually an animal, from memory. If it is a model, she can be captivated for hours, translating the pose into something extraordinary, as though she is able to identify the emotion signified in the model's stance – be it arrogance, moodiness, melancholy – and can push it past its limit into another dimension. While her strokes are broad and deft, she understands the power of detail, working quickly and intuitively to recreate not only what lies before her, but what exists in her mind's eye, far beyond. As though, he thinks, she understands innately what Proust meant when he said: 'Don't be afraid of going too far – that is where the truth resides.'

But there are not always models. And her refusal to tackle the still life is a problem. He decides not to discuss it with her in front of everybody else. There is no telling what effect it may have, either on her or on the all-too-interested group.

'Zara, would you stop by my office this afternoon? I need to discuss some aspects of the curriculum with you.'

She looks blank.

'About two o'clock? After lunch?'

She gives an almost imperceptible nod.

39

'Is that a yes?' he asks gently, the way one would coax a shy child.

She nods again.

The class ends a few minutes early, just before lunch. Time for one of the pleasures of his week: lunch with his secretary. Trudy arrived at the school a couple of years ago. At the time, she was married to a professional golfer and new in the Cape. Her husband, when not practising his swing, was invariably on tour. After several bouts of tears, he and his pretty little wife decided that she should get a job to help her pass the time. She applied for the job at the Jake Coleman International School of Fine Art, and started work the day after her interview. Nine days later she was sleeping with her boss. Within a year her husband had left her for a Brazilian air hostess. Today, thanks to a generous guilt-edged settlement, she can still afford not to work. But that would mean she would never see Jake. Which, of course, is out of the question.

Jake likes her. He really does. She is perfect for the job. She has an undemanding, sweet and compliant nature. Not to mention a body handcrafted for sin, and the wardrobe to match. Deep down he believes that every man deserves a Trudy. Someone who organises the details of his life, while dressing for him, laughing at his jokes and generally relieving the tension. Trudy is a lady of many talents, no doubt about that. If only he could think of a tactful way to get her to stop calling his house. Shouldn't be too difficult. Jake has always prided himself on being particularly good at lying to women. Is that wrong? he wonders. After all, he only tells them what they want to hear. It's an act of kindness really. Their ears exquisitely crafted to hear only what their sweet romantic souls can digest. Their ears . . . He sighs. He loves a beautiful, feminine ear.

Today she looks particularly attractive: svelte and sophisticated. Even coming in from the wind, her cropped ash-blonde hair accentuates her fine features and complements her olive skin and green-apple eyes. Everything about Trudy is precise. Her Virgoan eye for detail and her crispness soothes and neatens the often frayed edges of his unpredictable creative world.

And yet it was none of these things that attracted him to her in the first place. It was finding her one afternoon, her square, black-framed reading glasses halfway down her straight little nose, reading a Belgian art magazine, one of the selection he keeps scattered on coffee tables at reception. Her head was bent – her neck a perfect curve, a small pearl in the soft lobe of her perfect ear, the finest baby hair glowing delicate as dust in the after-noon light. Her lips were slightly parted, her brows slightly tensed. He could see from where he was watching that she was focused on an article written about him on page seventy-three.

She had been so shy at first. Averting her green eyes whenever he looked at her. And sincere. She hardly knew anything about painting, but she longed to learn. She would ask him question after question, and then suddenly blush. 'You must think me so ignorant.' And then their lovemaking. The 'Please don't leave me', whispered like a prayer as he lies spent, still inside her.

With pleasure he watches her walk towards him. Outwardly, she has a powerful womanly confidence. She knows the difference shoes with a little heel make to the swing of her gait. She knows the right shade of lipstick to apply, and now that she has learned the ropes, she knows how to look at him in a way that can set his blood alight. She also has the finest ankles he has ever seen.

Lunches are usually a kind of foreplay. They would sit sipping white wine and swapping food, their fingers intermittently interlacing. They would make suggestive innuendos in low voices, while under the table she would move her insistent stocking-clad toes up his legs. He does not remember ever having a real conversation with her about anything, but that is hardly the point. If ever he were to get so far as to think about it, he would inevitably come to the conclusion that Trudy is not supposed to be about anything real. She is fantasy at its least complicated. A concept.

Not that he doesn't think about her. He does. Of course he does! There are occasions when, climbing into bed at night, he imagines her slipping between her crisp cotton sheets, a mazagine sliding to the floor long after she has fallen asleep. But not that often. It is not his business. On the odd occasion when he does become the victim of her frustration, he ascribes it to PMT and keeps a low profile until she is over it. Till she comes quietly, sweetly, swollen-eyed, like a soft animal wanting to be held.

Today she is picking a friend up at the airport, so any lazy afternoon dalliance will have to be put on hold. Damn. He takes her back to the school to pick up her car and lock his office.

It is only after he has given her one last pat on the bottom, and walks towards his office that he suddenly remembers his appointment with Zara. *Shit!* He looks at his watch; he is an hour and a half late. She must have left ages ago. He is about to lock his office door and leave, shaking his head at his own forgetfulness, when something, some curious instinct, causes him to stop and quickly check inside. He turns the handle and without entering the room, surveys the desk, the two writing chairs and the armchair. In a shaft of afternoon light, a figure lies curled up on the large chair, asleep.

Perhaps he can attribute it to the excesses of lunch, but there is no telling how long he stares at this vision. Perhaps again, it is the wine, or even the coffee, but he feels a strong sensation pass through his body; a shortage of breath, a shudder of blood to the chest. Eventually, he enters the room and, checking that nobody is approaching, carefully closes the door behind him. Treading as softly as possible he stands before her. He must wake her. Yes, he surely must wake her. And yet when he opens his mouth, no words will come. His body feels slow and disconnected. Heavy, as in dream state. The computer drones quietly in the corner. Outside, the wind screams. A starling hops onto the window sill, but he does not see it. Flapping its wings it calls raucously to its mate, but he does not hear it. With brows bent, his sole focus has converged on this: this mirage before him.

Her body, as tall as he is when she is standing, is curled with feline grace into a surprisingly compact little ball. The shapeless skirt has fallen to the side, revealing the length of her legs. He hardly dares breathe. His eyes assimilate every last detail: a battered shoe hanging from the smooth arch of her foot. The tiny soft hairs on her legs. The gentle curve of her shoulder, where the oversized bottle-green T-shirt has fallen away. The outlined arc of a breast. And then her face. That sleep can be so revealing. That it can have pulled back the covers of her savage impenetrability to show this deep serenity, this translucence beneath the passivity. He kneels down in front of her. Leans forward and inhales: she smells like the rain. To touch her, just once. Should he dare? Closing his eyes, he puts out his hand, curling his fingers in front of her face to feel the warm vapour of her breath between his fingers.

'Zara,' he whispers.

And then her scream.

He jumps back, but already her nails have moved like fire through his skin. Already the chair is knocked over. And before he can get to his feet, she has fled. He runs to the balcony, calling, but she has gone. He puts a hand to his burning cheek, feeling the blood flow warm and sticky over his fingers.

'Zara!' he shouts. 'Zara!'

But as though to confirm that it is merely a dream, the word rushes back, hollow and mocking, along the empty corridors.

SIX

LEAH SEPTEMBER IS always early to rise. Even on the weekends, through sheer force of habit, she is up and active by six o'clock. This morning, Sunday, is no different. Goiya staggered into bed in the early hours of the morning, shouting invectives intermingled with odd lines of song, before lying back, folding his hands on his chest and snoring with conviction within seconds.

'Bastard,' she mumbled, half asleep. There was a time when, under similar circumstances, a small hint of a smile might have twisted one side of the yin-yang mouth. But not any more.

Hours later, as she stands in the first light before the broken piece of mirror, and notes that the black eye has turned a grotesque yellow, the bile of resentment burns in her throat. Raindrops like stones sting the tin roof and batter the window pane; a low cloud obscures the mountain. With jaws clenched she digs in a patched bag for some old, caked make-up and with a small sponge and some water sets about repairing the damage.

It's not that she wants to impress these people – these fokken mad people who insist on interfering with her life. God Himself must know, that's all she needs right now. White do-gooders. It's all a blerrie nonsense. She becomes more vigorous with the make-up, slapping it on thicker and thicker, wincing every now and then.

But what can she do? If she refuses to go she will be rude. Not to mention the movie-star performance Blom will throw. She sighs and shakes her head at the thought. But if she must go, she will not have them feeling sorry for her. She will accept their hospitality for a few hours. But over her dead body will she accept their pity.

In the cottage where she will visit in a few hours' time, the mother lies awake next to her child. Again Zara's nightmares have rent the night. Again she has woken to the sound of her daughter's breath becoming increasingly laboured, turning into short, dry gasps, her small hands tensed and flailing. Again she has taken the child in her arms and softly asked, 'What is it? Zara, Zara . . . *ce n'est qu'un rêve*. It's a dream, *ma petite*. Come, what is it? Tell me.'

Above the hammering of rain on the roof, she could only just make out the single response: 'Dead birds.'

'Dead birds? What dead birds?' she probed.

But inevitably there was no answer. The child was still caught in the dark clutches of sleep. And in the morning, she would not remember.

And then there were the other nights, when turning in her sleep she would instinctively feel Zara's absence. Lifting the weight of her head from the pillow, she would see her at the window, staring up at the stars, her long hair almost touching the hem of her nightie.

'What are you doing?' she would whisper. Laika's tail would thump lazily on the wooden floor, to indicate his inclusion.

But there was never any reply. Quite soon she realised that Zara, transfixed by the night sky, was not awake.

She had started to realise that she must be very careful which stories she read Zara; her identification with the story was so marked that she often couldn't sleep for fear. She drew witches with claws and blood dripping from their fingers. She drew death without understanding what it really meant, muttering inaudibly to herself, her eyes dark and intense. But the worst was always if she had seen a dead animal that day. A cat run over, a bird with its neck broken. This seemed to break her heart as though she had lost a family member. How would she ever survive the force of the world without any skin?

For a while, she was convinced that Zara's over-empathetic attachment to animals was due to a lack of friends of her own age. She had even tried sending Zara to the local pre-school. What a disaster *that* had been.

It had only lasted a week. The school had 'Valleyland Junior Primary' in brown and gold on the metal sign on the gate. And VJP on the pocket of Zara's brown-and-white uniform. The uniform with the tunic which hung oversized and stiff, with a huge hem, over her kneecaps.

'Do I have to wear it every day?' Zara had asked.

'Yes,' she had replied.

'*Every day?*' Zara could not believe it. She hated it! Out of the corner of her eye, Camille watched her thinking it through, brow furrowed, muttering under her breath. The same brown tunic with white shirt. Every brown-and-white school day. For the rest of her life.

From the start things had gone badly. From what she could piece together, at recess a band of pigtailed conspirators had circled Zara, waving tiny fingers at her in knowing reprehension, gathering up their accusations in an evil little clump.

'You have no dad . . .' the ringleader seemed to have chanted. The others had apparently copied her, 'And

47

you never *did* have either . . . which my big brother says means you're a bastard.'

'What's a bastard?' Zara had later asked her. 'Does it have to wear a uniform?'

But what Zara did understand soon enough, from the superior giggles of this miniature coven, was that she was excluded. So while the other children at the school would play on jungle gyms and slides, pairing off and holding hands with newly made best friends, she would head for a grassy corner close to the staffroom, where she would sit cross-legged, drawing. That was until she was found out.

Ah, Mrs Meijer, Camille remembers wryly. The teacher with the beetle-shaped body and a nose for delinquency. A sharp one like a triangle. The teacher who believed that bad behaviour could be stamped out if caught early enough. The same one who had found somewhere in the Bible that the heart was evil. And had been known to say that nowhere was this more clearly seen than in the behaviour of children. Apparently, her views were well known in the Christian community: she believed the evil heart could be redeemed only by the Saviour and by discipline. Especially the latter. That was her special calling. The one she would have to answer for one day, when she stood before the Almighty. No doubt she was thinking about this very thing, about this enormous responsibility and duty that rested on her ample shoulders, when her sin-detecting radar must have tuned into the disrespectful lilt of Zara's voice singing its way into the staffroom window.

'What song were you singing?' Camille had been curious to know later.

'An English one. The one from the records. Pappi's record with the English songs:

'Now Ebenezer
Thought he was Julia Seizure
So they sent him to a ho-oh-home . . .'

The teacher, obedient to the voice of the Lord, conscientiously tracked its owner down. And found Zara modelling a cow from a piece of blue plasticine.

'And so they gave him
Medicinal compounds
Now he's the empah-rah
Of Rome . . .'

'This is out of bounds, little girl. Now move it. Go to the playground where you belong.'

Zara had blatantly ignored her, the teacher told Camille.

'Is that true, Zara?' she later asked.

'No,' said Zara. 'I just didn't answer her, that's all. I just went away.'

It seems she had walked apprehensively back to the playground, trying to find a tree, a bush, somewhere she could hide. But they had found her again, and the jeering had continued.

'They said I was bad because I didn't believe in God.'

'So what did you do?' Camille wanted to know.

'I said I did believe in God. I even know His name. His name is Neruda.'

But the children had scorned her even further.

'So then I went to the toilet,' she said.

'And then?'

'And then I went back to where the teacher found me. I thought if I didn't sing she wouldn't mind.'

But the teacher did mind. And viewed the matter as

gross insubordination. The mother would have to be called in.

'Your child has interactive problems,' she had told Camille. 'She does not mix with other children. Refuses to participate. And is blatantly disobedient.'

'Refuses? Er, that is a strong word, Mrs Meijer. Zara is not that kind of child. It's possible she just chooses to do something else, yes?'

Mrs Meijer was clearly not in the habit of being questioned. Or disagreed with. And, Camille felt, took particular exception that the heathen woman doing so spoke in a foreign accent. Camille could tell that differences made her feel unsure and uncomfortable. She seemed quick to condemn anything she did not understand with the full force of her godly judgement.

Camille watched her fold baguette-shaped arms across her torso, take a deep breath through a tiny vein-spattered nose and take a step forward. ' "Refuses . . . Chooses" . . . What's the difference? She's being stubborn and naughty. And seeing as she has no father to take the matter in hand, it's up to you, I'm afraid, Miss Pascal.'

'Ah! About this, we agree then, Mrs Meijer.' Camille's voice, usually so melodic, was clipped. Like music from a waltz played slightly staccato. 'It is my responsibility. And it must stay this way.'

Beneath her composure, Camille burned hot ice. For the first time since she had arrived in the Cape, she did not notice the grandeur of the mountain shimmering in the heat of the day as she walked back to the cottage. Was unaware of the sun throwing warmth into her dark hair, touching the prominence of her high cheekbones. She found her lips moving and tightening with each word that had been said. And more so, with those that had not been said. Her smooth, slightly swaying gait swung into a march.

And that was the school. Zara had never gone back. She had stayed with her mother, and her grandfather, and her dog, and her world of make-believe and animals, right up until Blom had dropped out of the sky, a gift. And still Camille worries. Zara has been a paradox since she was born. She did not speak a word for the first three and a half years. Not a word! They were convinced she was mute. And then one day, without warning or hesitation, she looked up from where she was playing and, wanting her pencil crayons, asked, 'Where are my colours?' Even with Blom she would sing and play with childlike abandon, and yet never give too much of herself away. Already she has developed an extraordinary sense of privacy. An instinctive form of self-protection that lends her dignity, a composure, way beyond her years. And the fact that she seems oblivious to it makes it all the more fascinating to watch.

Only in one respect does this change. When it comes to drawing and painting Zara is quite different. She can keep herself busy for hours, confidently creating worlds of wonder, worlds of terror. Safe and content in a fabulous freedom that is drawn from a talent so innate she herself neither questions nor marvels at it. Her drawings could be softer than rain; violent as lightning. They were always of animals.

How beautiful things are when they sleep, she thinks, especially children. Zara's nightmare must have ended; now she floats on a pillow of slow and sweet breath, her purposeful little fingers curled. She can remember being that age. *Was she too that small and precise?* Memories, faces, bob softly through her mind like petals on water. It was then when she met her half-brother, Juergen, her only sibling, for the first time. He was twenty-one. Had lived in Argentina with his mother since he was fifteen. They shared a father, their papa. Juergen came out to France to visit for ten days for the first time in seven years. The day they brought him home from the airport, she became ill, probably from excitement. Only hours before he was due to arrive she came down with a terrible fever. But they brought him straight back to the house, where she was lying in bed, only her eyes peering above the sheets, watching and waiting, for her brother. When he came through the door, olive-skinned and beaming, she pulled the sheets over her head. And Juergen laughed and said what was this all about, this being sick on the day her brother comes all the way from Argentina to meet her for the first time. And she didn't move. She couldn't look at him. She just kept those sheets right over her head. So he said let's make a deal. You don't have to show me your face, if you stick out your hand from under the sheet. Not both hands, just one. This seemed like a fair compromise, and quite soon her small clammy fist was being held in her brother's warm grip. Juergen. Now married with five children and farming in Argentina. She followed him relentlessly during those ten days. He carried her on his shoulders. Sat her on his lap. Told her marvellous stories. Taught her how to make *tortillas*. And then ten days later, he left. She remembers the trip to the airport. He was wearing a red shirt, soft. He smelled like pink musk sweets. And she could not speak, all the way on the train, for fear she would cry. And she could not hold his hand, nor catch his eye. She had simply to concentrate very hard and keep swallowing even though it made her twitch and her head sore. And all the way she kept it up. All the way. Even when they reached the airport and a calm woman's voice came over the loudspeaker calling passengers for their flight. Juergen shook his father's hand, then hugged him, then kissed him on both cheeks, then hugged him again. But before he could drop to his haunches to look his little sister in the eye one last time, she had gone. As though something in her chest had snapped and she had been catapulted to the other side of the building, to somewhere in the crowds, *anywhere,* away from the soft shirt. She hid among the arms and legs and handbags and elbows at the window, and watched him walking away. Watched him turning to look back once or twice, as though he had a question, his red shirt billowing in the wind, then toss his old backpack over his shoulder and walk on. Could he see her, a small convulsive child beating her hands against the thick airport window panes, feeling their dull, separating force. Could he hear her cry? Is that why he began walking faster, to escape from her pain? Till the fat white stair tube had swallowed him into the giant, squat, whirring machine?

And so it is with loss, she thinks; absence is only half the pain, complete powerlessness the rest. How was he to know, her big half-brother Juergen, that the man she would later love would leave the same way? The grand themes of our lives a wheel ever turning.

At ten o'clock, Leah September walks silently down the road and across the field till she reaches the cottage on the lower side of Meneer Smit's farm. Her child's fist gripped in one hand, in the other an umbrella with two bent tines, making it collapse on the one side. The child's mother is standing at the door.

'Hello,' she calls.

'Hello . . .' Leah is about to add 'Merrem', but stops.

Zara suddenly appears at her mother's side, staring silently at the arrival of Blom and her mother. Unblinking, she eyes the web of frosty raindrops twinkling on Blom's buoyant curls. *A fairy crown. Must be.*

'Come inside. Come out of the rain.' Camille Pascal holds the door open.

The room is warm. A fire hisses and fusses in the grate. The smell of baking floods every corner. Blom tears away from her mother's grip and races across to the stove.

'What's cooking?' she demands.

'Cakes,' Zara replies. 'Fairy cakes; *you* should know.'

Without the child's hand in hers, Leah stands awkwardly, the toes of her right foot slightly turned in. She watches Camille move towards the old oven, the bright blue apron wrapped tightly around her small waist.

'Take a seat,' Camille smiles and motions with her arm, as she bends and removes the cupcakes from the stove.

Leah bites her cheek. She moves stiffly to the old leather chair. Suddenly notices the old man in the other, asleep with his chin on his chest, and gives a little jump.

'It's okay,' says Camille. 'That's my father. He often falls asleep when we have a fire.'

Leah gives a little nod. She sits at the end corner of the chair, with her knees together and her feet slightly apart.

'Can I help?' she asks Camille.

'Yes, I'm going to bring the cakes over there, and we can all ice them.'

Leah watches Camille closely: Haai, that way she has

of walking; the sway of her hips mos, like there's a hundred men in the room. Even the way she wears her clothes, that red skirt and tight black jersey, showing off her body like nobody's business! It's no wonder people talk. She feels the gap in her own front teeth with her tongue, unconsciously tries to stretch her dress over her dark and dimpled knees.

'When do you want to see the concert?' Blom wants to know. Her mother does not answer.

'Let's ice these first,' says Camille, setting down a tray of cakes and a bowl of icing with spatulas and spoons on the little table in the middle of the floor.

Enticed by the warm vanilla smell, the dog rises from his spot in front of the fire, shakes the sleep out, then comes over to look, wagging his tail.

'No, Laika. Not now.' Camille has to push him firmly away.

After Camille has iced the first fairy cake, Leah takes a spatula and ices another. The children each try to ice one, but before long shovel the cake and a spoonful of icing into their mouths.

'Blom!' hisses Leah.

'Listen to that rain on the roof,' says Camille.

'Sounds like popcorn,' says Zara.

'Why don't you two go and get ready for the concert?' suggests Camille, rising to fetch a pot of coffee.

The two disappear into the alcove where Camille and Zara sleep.

'How are things at the farm?' Camille calls across to Leah.

'Oh, s'fine. Same old, same old, you know.' She gives a small smile, without opening her mouth.

Camille pours strong coffee into a pottery mug and passes the sugar.

The children reappear wearing Camille's lipstick. Zara shakes Pappi's arm till he grunts and wakes, and the concert begins.

Out of the corner of her good eye, Leah watches Camille. What the hell is this woman doing encouraging friendship with a Coloured family? It's asking for trouble, that's what.

Suddenly the children stop. 'At the window,' says Zara to Blom. 'It's Pieter.'

Pappi stretches and makes his way over to the window, to find a small boy crouching under the eaves. He undoes the latch and with a push releases the rain-soaked wood.

'Tell him to fokoff,' says Blom.

'Blom . . .' Her mother winces; shakes her head.

'Tell him to come inside!' insists Zara. 'He knows "Au Clair de la Lune". He must sing.'

The old man opens the door and greets the small boy in the green corduroys and the navy sweater. 'Allo,' he says.

'Hello, Meneer,' the reply is muffled. The boy watches him from deep under his eyebrows.

'Can you sing "Au Clair de la Lune"?' the old man asks. His face is masked with the gravity of a judge.

'Hey?' Pieter does not understand the accent.

The old man repeats himself slowly.

'No, Meneer. I mean, I don't know, Meneer.'

'He's lying,' Zara calls out. 'He can. Tell him to come.'

'Tell him to fokoff!' insists Blom.

'Come, young man,' the old man offers. Then, more insistent: 'Come, *petit*. It's raining.'

The boy scuttles inside, his veldskoens bringing with them ample evidence of the soft, muddy earth.

Leah's mouth is tight. This has turned from bad to worse.

'Haai, Tannie,' he greets her softly.

'What are you doing here, Pieter?' Leah is shaking her head. This is really asking for trouble. If his parents knew . . . Jesus, that snooty bitch mother of his would go *ballies*! 'You want trouble, Pieter?'

'No, Tannie.' He looks down.

Zara takes his hand. 'First, sing like we showed you. Otherwise no cake.'

'It's *our* cake,' glares Blom, before taking her place in front of the fireplace to sing.

Leah clasps tense fingers.

Blom looks first at Zara, then at Pieter, then gives the count of three to lead them into song. This is repeated several times. Each time one child misses the cue, until finally Camille steps in.

'Let me count to three, okay? One, two, three . . .'

The children launch into the song. Zara stares ahead unabashedly, her clear voice repeating the words of the song she has grown up singing. Blom sings with exaggerated concentration, taking deep breaths between lines and swaying her body in time to the song. And Pieter sings very softly, looking down at his veldskoens all the while.

At the end of the song, the old man starts to clap.

'Bravo! *Magnifique!* Bravo!'

Camille lifts her hands and claps as noisily as she can. Even Leah, releasing her grip, politely joins in.

The children descend on the fairy cakes and start arguing about who got the song wrong. Camille leans towards Leah.

'What's the matter?' she asks Leah quietly. 'Why shouldn't the boy be here?'

Leah pretends not to hear. She clasps her hands in front of her again, digging her fingertips so clawingly into the back of the opposite hands that her brown skin shows milky pink indentations.

'Leah,' repeats Camille, 'what is wrong with the boy being here?'

Leah shifts her torso in discomfort, then shakes her head and sighs.

'His parents don't like it. His mother's a funny one.'

'Don't like what?'

Leah gives a little laugh, without moving her lips too much so as not to show the gap in her front teeth, and shifts in her seat.

'You haven't been here long, have you?'

'Not too long. A few years. Why?'

'You come from where?' Leah is curious to know.

'France.'

'Ah. I never been. But here is not like France.' She enjoys the authority that this small knowledge affords. 'Here, people like the Smits – Meneer Smit? The owner of the farm?'

Camille nods.

'People like them like to keep their washing separate. Or at least when it suits them.' Her eyes harden. 'And you don't mix white with coloured washing, if you unnerstand.'

Camille listens quietly, pouring out more coffee into each of the pottery mugs, while Leah continues.

'But that kid is lonely. I see him all day long on his bicycle, up en down the street, while the mother is out at one of her bridge parties or lunches or whatever. And the father doesn't pitch up at home in the day either.'

Suddenly Blom gives a loud wail.

'What's the matter?' Camille turns to ask.

'She says I'm not a fairy,' sobs Blom.

Zara stares at them. Her dark eyes, resolute and opaque. She does not say a word.

'Zara?' Camille repeats with intent.

'And now she doesn't want to be my friend,' howls Blom with renewed dramatic devastation.

'Oh, I'm sure that's not true. Zara! That's not true, is it?'

Zara nods. 'I want a fairy, not a friend,' comes the reply. 'She can't fly.' And with that she leaves the room.

The rain has stopped for a moment. Even so, rainwater still drips like a metronome into the green plastic bucket in the corner. Leah shuffles her feet, then shifts awkwardly in her seat. Blom sniffs, and Pieter stares at his shoes. Eventually, the old man stands up. 'I think I take Laika for a walk. You come?' he asks Pieter and Blom. Like the dog, wagging its tail at the mention of his name, the children do not need to be asked twice.

Camille puts her head into their tiny bedroom. As expected, Zara is sprawled out on the bed, her crayons all about her, drawing. She thinks about encouraging her to join the other children for the walk, then thinks better of it and returns to the stove to boil some more water for tea.

She glances across at Leah, who is unconsciously touching the swelling around her eye.

'Have you lived here long?' Camille asks.

'Here in the valley?'

'Yes.'

'Goiya's lived here for all his life, his brothers and his mother's mother *ensovoorts*. Me, I's born in Cape Town. You know District Six?'

'Not really.'

'That's because it's not there any more. It's gone.'

'What happened?'

'Oh, the guvverment decide they want to clean up the city. And the Coloureds is part of the rubbish they want to clean up, you know. So they bring the bulldozers one day and peoples is crying and throwing themselves in front of the bulldozers, you know, and they don't care. Nee wat. Mos put us in the lorrie and take us to the Cape Flats. To "Lavender Hill", and places like this which got sweet English names, and that's all they got. So I decide no, bugger this, and I come to stay with my cousin who lives here by a wine farm. And she get me a job, and then I meet Goiya, and I'm only twenty-something, and we get married, and he's a drunk bastard even then, and I stay.' Her fingers move subconsciously over the bruise around her eye once again.

'That looks painful.' Camille's voice is soft. The longing to be a part of the healing process again rises in her chest. When she first arrived here, she vowed she would find a nursing job as soon as Zara was settled. But that was taking longer than expected. What's more, there were no hospitals for miles.

Leah does not answer.

'Can I make you a little cold pack for that, while everyone is out? It will bring down the swelling. I can add some mint too; I have some in the garden. That often helps.'

'Moenie worry nie. It's okay.' Leah's eyes grow darker.

'I won't hurt you, really. I'm a nurse . . .'

Leah suddenly stands up. For a second she feels an urge to violate the perfection of this woman; her softness, her serenity. She wants to demand to know whether she has the first idea *what* she is talking about.

With her little walk and her little cakes and her accent and her daughter; everything so *sweet*. She may be a little lonely, away from her fancy foreign country, and what does she expect if she goes about dressed like that, but what does she really know about hardship? What does she know about what helps, and what doesn't help? After all, hers is hardly a face that has ever had a fist through it!

'"Help"? That will take more than mint,' her lips are tight. 'Or a nurse. I must get home. Thank you for asking me.'

The cottage suddenly feels very empty. Camille sinks into a chair. Why did she ever do this? Bring everything across to this land of angry, misplaced strangers? Had she really felt *that* desperate that she had to pack it all in a few suitcases and leave her country and her job in the French country hospital for good? Little Zara struggling to get along, to fit in. The little boy that has come over not allowed to ease his loneliness because his mother deems the company 'inappropriate'. At least there is this: they need never feel alone in their isolation, if that can be considered a consolation. Not here in this land of the walking wounded. Not here where the wound seems to have so many faces. Of course, she must concede, the French are not particularly friendly to strangers either. But in France the unfriendliness has its roots in their perceptions of superiority, not inferiority. In perfection – or at least perceived perfection – not brokenness. It is a strange form of patriotism. She smiles ruefully, thinking of the homeless man in her hometown in France, who carried his only worldly possessions in a supermarket trolley, a French flag tied to one corner. How welcome that arrogance would be right now.

An hour later the old man can be seen slowly making his way up the pathway. Pieter is riding his red bicycle and Blom is holding the old man's hand. They do not ask about Zara at first, and cram a few more fairy cakes into their mouths. It is Pieter who quietly takes the last cake into the bedroom, before he and Blom leave, scattering like dice in different directions. As promised, they do not mention that they have learned words like 'jockey', and 'trifecta'.

SEVEN

THEY ARE ALREADY late. Maria glances at her gold watch.

'Come *on,* Jake! They're going to be waiting. What's the matter with you?'

He has lost track of time in the bath. In fact, he has lost track of time, period.

'Huh?' he appears, pink and dishevelled, tucking his shirt in.

'Comb your hair, Jake,' Maria scolds. 'My God! What happened to your face?'

This time, he cannot think of an answer at all.

'Hmm,' is all he can muster, returning to the bedroom to find a comb, a brush, whatever. She bustles in behind him, her face growing flushed.

'Jake, answer me, what happened to your face?'

'I dunno,' he mumbles.

'Don't give me that. What's got into you all of a sudden? Answer me, goddammit.'

'Maria, give me a break,' he says with measured patience. 'I've had an awful day. I don't want to talk about it. I don't want to go tonight. I'm only going for you. Now leave me alone.'

'I won't stand for it, Jake. You can't arrive home with scratches all over your face and not give me an explanation. I suppose it was some woman . . .' She starts gathering steam.

But it is he who explodes, picking up the car keys and hurling them to the ground with such force that a piece of one of the keys splinters off.

'Jesus, Maria! Will you lay off?'

They arrive at the Bryants in silence. The meal, impeccably presented as always, will no doubt follow the usual pattern: cocktails in the drawing room before dinner, light classics filtering through as the guests arrange themselves, like chess pieces, in advantageous positions in the room. Hand-picked for utmost effect, there are usually at least two or three celebrities to garnish the affair. 'Just a sprinkling, darling,' gushes Cecily Charlston-Bryant to Maria. 'Never hurts to network.'

Jake is never without a small circle that manages to manoeuvre itself according to some unspoken politics of looks and glances within his ambit.

'Jake Coleman. The painter,' people confirm in hushed whispers behind their fluted glasses. Jake usually pretends not to hear.

The low hum of conversation just above the music. An occasional laugh. The clink of ice and glass. A typical soirée at Cecily's. So why does it suddenly feel so different to him? Surreal. As though he is an observer, not a participant. With whiskey tumbler in hand, he circles the room absent-mindedly, ignoring the recognition, the smiles, the eyes following him. Several of his paintings hang in different parts of the room. He stops in front of each one, looking at them as though he has just seen them for the first time. He touches the scratches on his face. *What if she doesn't come back?*

At the far end of the room he stares at a painting he did ten years ago. A painting called *Malay Woman with Fishes*. He had taken the photo at first light in Kalk Bay, when the early fishing boats come back with their catch. First light and the sticky salt-thickened air and the wind bringing the smell of fish. Leathery men hauling nets of snoek, still slithering and thrashing, onto plastic crates waiting gaping on the shore. And women there to meet them. The one he photographed middle-aged. Swaddled in poverty. Colourful rags about her head. A makeshift skirt and top and a shawl to cover her upper body and sprawling bosom. She was not drunk. Yet she did not walk, she staggered, her brown feet flip-flapping in old takkies, no shoelaces, along the rough stones and glinting broken glass and lilac mussel shells. Once she had negotiated her fee amid a windmill of arms and toothless shouting, she staggered back towards him, holding two fish by the tail, long and silver, one in each hand. It was then he took the photograph. Captured her face, ochre and purple, contorted with the raw struggle of living. And started painting it the same day.

He had only just met Maria. Was still struggling to make ends meet. And yet if he thinks about her response to the painting it seems ludicrous now.

'Love the colours!' she said. 'It's so *moving*. You've really captured the *feel*.'

But when she flogged it to Cecily Charlston-Bryant for R10,000 he forgave her. And painted an entire Malay series. His bank balance was growing for the first time. He had a new confidence and it showed. But he stopped taking risks. Borrowing ideas from other painters: the dreamscapes of Klee, the floating lovers of Chagall, whatever seemed popular at the time. His enthusiasm was contagious. *Everybody loves a winner*.

Maria cannot believe it. In public Jake has always elected to show a disaffected nonchalance about his work. Compliments are usually received with a shrug and a smile, as though his talent were a slight embarrassment; one he would prefer not to discuss. But tonight he does not seem to care at all about 'his audience'. In fact, he is behaving as though he is the only person in the room. Had they been on speaking terms she could have adjusted his behaviour. As it is, she can merely observe with seething disapproval.

'Paintings look vaguely familiar, Jake?' Cecily oozes, trying to catch his eye.

Whether he chooses not to hear, or really does not hear, is hard to say.

'Jake!' Maria hisses. 'Cecily is talking to you.'

'Hmm? Really. Oh, hello, Cecily.' His smile is automatic. 'How are you?'

But before she can launch into an answer he has glided past her.

Maria is apologetic. 'He hasn't been himself lately.'

'What happened to his face?'

'His face? Oh, that. Cat.'

'Never knew you had one.'

'Dr Coleman! Damn good to see you. How you doing, sport?'

Patrick Le Roux, the gynaecologist, is more difficult to avoid. Two minutes of his company – his beaming, booming, backslapping camaraderie – is like finding yourself in a hall of horrors, with no escape except to nod your head as though it is loose, smile, try to say something amusing, and then excuse yourself to go to the bathroom. Patrick Le Roux owns several of his paintings, and is the quintessential cultural *parvenu*. He is frequently seen in the social pages of social magazines pictured with various artists, writers, poets, painters, musicians. He name-drops whenever he can. Considers himself a man of distinctive exotic tastes and expansive political sensibilities because he has a girlfriend 'of colour'. Lily, with her chiselled features, caramel skin and modulated voice, is a television presenter and, in Jake's opinion, Patrick's sole redeeming feature.

'How are you, Jake?'

'Ah, the lovely Lily.' He kisses her on the cheek. For a moment he almost feels his old self again.

'What happened to your cheek, old boy?' This, with a resounding backslap, and suddenly an evening that can't become worse, does.

'Oh, I really don't know. Cut myself shaving, I suppose.'

Perhaps it is his natural elevation, but when Patrick Le Roux roars with laughter, it is always louder and longer-lasting than anyone else.

'Cut yourself shaving? What kind of razor is that then? Shaped like a knitting needle?' More laughter and backslapping.

'Meet Arnie McKenzie,' he says. 'Arnie's a surgeon. Spends six months here and six months in Santa Barbara.'

He shakes hands with Arnie. 'Sounds like the best of both worlds.'

'Oh God, yeah, tell me about it.'

'And the best part,' interjects Patrick, 'is that he earns in dollars, so with our economy he ends up getting an increase almost every week!'

Patrick and Arnie appear to find this hilarious. Once they have wiped the tears from their cheeks, Patrick takes his arm.

'Now listen, old boy, off to Switzerland in a few months. Skiing with some French writers and popping in to see good old Henri.'

'Who is he again?' Jake smiles, knowing it irritates

Patrick that he should forget that he has such a treasured acquaintance.

'Henri? Sport, he's a well-known Swiss philosopher! I *must* have mentioned him before. He's a longstanding friend of the family.'

Of course you've mentioned him before, Jake thinks. You mention him as often as you can.

'So I was thinking, sport, how about knocking up a quick masterpiece for us to take over as a gift?' More laughter at his own excellent wit.

Jake smiles politely.

'No, seriously, old chap, I mean it. It would be *wonderful* to take over a recent Coleman. We travel first class, you know. It would be dead easy to take it on the plane. Come now, what are you working on? Spill the beans.'

'What did you have in mind?' Jake redirects the conversation.

'Oh really, I don't care what it is. As long as it's a Coleman it doesn't matter, does it? No really, I don't care a bean! Why not do something like . . . that?' He points to the nearest of Jake's paintings. An abstract blue vase with flowers and various geometric shapes. He had taken the idea from a painting he'd seen in a restaurant in San Francisco. It had strong overtones of Matisse.

'I'll see what I can do,' Jake mutters and moves on.

He wanders across to the mantelpiece over the opulent fireplace. Rests his drink on an antique gold coaster, and picks up a rather unusual piece of pottery and examines it closely.

'It's a tea bowl. Lovely, isn't it?' Maria appears to be following him. As though he can't be trusted not to make a fool of himself.

He continues to turn the piece over in his hands. 'Yes, I like it. Can't say why for sure, but it does have a certain charm.'

'Cecily and Roland have quite a bit of this stuff. Apparently, the man who makes it has been invited tonight. Not sure who, or where, he is.' She swivels her eyes around the room.

'You should get him to give you some samples for consignment. For the gallery.'

'Good idea.' Now she knows he's not himself. Jake never recommends anyone else's work for the gallery.

'I'll see what I can do. Oh God, there's Juanita. Try to be polite, Jake.'

There are three things Juanita Le Grange feels compelled to tell all she meets: the first is that she has a PhD; the second, that she is a communist, and the third, that she married a man who died in 'the struggle'. Jake has often noted that her strictly communist lifestyle seems to include a few minor incongruencies: a ten-bedroom mansion overlooking Camps Bay; a black Mercedes sports car; and several first-class trips overseas each year. Not to mention a number of his paintings; she is always first on Maria's list when there is an exhibition.

It somehow doesn't bother her that she is known as 'the cashmere communist' in many circles, or that she has been quoted saying, 'I hate capitalism but there's nothing wrong with capital,' in *Style* magazine. She is known to support any cause providing the right publicity is at hand. She could easily have been a politician, he thinks.

'Jake, how are you?' She extends a gloved paw towards him, her fat little body swaddled in folds of silk. She has peroxided her very short hair. It does not suit her. 'Juanita.' He cannot even attempt a smile. Such a pity that such a pretty name is worn by such a woman. He doubts that it's real.

'When are you going to have another exhibition? I'm redoing my guest suite, and I'm looking for something stunning in green. As you know, I have many visiting academics staying with me, and occasionally the odd revolutionary. Time to upgrade their accommodation. It's the least I can do.'

'Of course.'

Maria sweeps in to the rescue.

'Juanita! How lovely to see you.' She deposits a noisy kiss on her fat, powdery cheek. 'Did I hear you asking Jake when we're having another exhibition? Isn't it funny, *everybody's* been asking the same question. Hear that, Jake? Everybody wants you, darling.' She turns back to Juanita. 'The truth is, we simply cannot keep up with the orders. And they are flowing in from overseas too. Collectors in Germany, France, even some former Russian royalty, believe it or not, all wanting a Coleman. Jake is so exhausted. He needs a break. All this really takes it out of him. He's been painting morning, noon and night. But as soon as he has a break, and does something extra special, we will give you a call.' She touches Juanita lightly on the arm, and lowers her voice. 'You know you are always on the top of our list when something special is in the offing. Very few people in this country know true art when they see it; the rest just pretend, and follow trends. But you are one of those few. And we treasure you dearly.'

She's good! Jake thinks as he walks away, trying not to smile. And this will get them all clamouring for more. If only he could paint a single brushstroke he felt happy with.

'Thank you,' he mouths to Maria with the smallest hint of a grin. The whiskey is smoothing the edges of his mood. He is starting to find the evening rather amusing. He wanders into an adjacent room, a study, and starts looking at the books.

'Good evening.' It is a man's voice, deep and measured and foreign.

Jake turns to find a large man of indeterminate age sitting in a chair, with a book in his hands.

'Good evening,' he replies. And then, taken off guard a little, adds, 'I'm sorry, I didn't mean to disturb you. I didn't know anyone was in here.'

'It's okay,' the hefty blond man smiled. 'It is not my house. You are free, like me, to be here.'

'Jake Coleman,' Jake holds out his hand.

'Mátyás,' he replies, putting his book on the table, and standing up to shake hands.

'Escaping the throng?' Jake asks.

'I'm no good at parties,' the large man smiles.

He is far taller and broader than Jake, dressed in an old cobalt-blue shirt and a pair of navy trousers.

'What is the accent?' Jake asks, squeezing his hand very firmly to compensate for the size discrepancy.

'Hungary originally. But I have lived here for some time. What about you? Are you from here?'

'Yes. Born 'n' bred Capetonian. You known Cecily and Roland long?'

'No, not really. They buy some of my pottery occasionally. So I suppose that makes them "clients".'

Just then, the bell rings for dinner.

'Ah, to the table,' says Jake.

The large man follows him in.

The table seats sixteen. People are carefully arranged and each place meticulously laid. Jake is relieved to find himself between Lily and Cecily, and even more relieved that Maria is at the other end. He can feel her watching him out of the corner of her eye; she probably senses how attractive he finds Lily. Although she too is starting to thaw, and say things are 'fabulous'. A good sign. She only says 'fabulous' when she's very happy or a little drunk. The large Hungarian in the blue shirt is seated alongside her. He does not appear to be a man of many words.

Candles, classical music and Cabernet, he notes. It's always the same. But the alcohol is slowly blunting his critical faculties and, comforted as always by the presence of beauty and praise, he relaxes into the ritual clink of glasses and the warm hum of conversation.

By the time they get into the car to drive home, his mood has shifted. He is gentle now. Subdued. He takes Maria's hand in the car, and listens to at least every third word.

'Turns out *he's* the potter who keeps missing appointments with me,' she says.

'Hmmmm. Who?'

'Mátyás. That big, blond man with the dark eyes, sitting next to me. He didn't pitch up for the appointment the other day either. The one I woke up particularly early for. He lives in Glencairn. I suppose it's quite a drive. But I've asked him to bring some work to the gallery, like you said. Did you see how casually he was dressed?'

'Maria?'

'Yes.'

'Do you remember when you first met me, the people who showed interest in my paintings were down-to-earth? Normal. They often came to exhibitions on their own, because they wanted to see the work, not because

72

it was the thing to do. Sometimes they brought a sketchpad and made notes, there were no trophy partners. Sometimes the women wore make-up, sometimes not. Sometimes shoes, sometimes not. What happened to them?'

'I don't know. They probably never had any money. Sweet as they were, of course. You would never have survived like that. You outgrew them, Jake, that's all.'

'Maybe they just liked what they saw then. And don't any more. Maybe they outgrew me?'

EIGHT

THE KNOCKING MUST have gone on for quite a while before she hears it. The night is wild; wind tugs at the tin roof first from this direction, then that. The knocking simply becoming part of the weather, rattling and desperate. It is the little sob between gusts that makes Laika lift his head and Camille get out of the bed where Zara lies warm and curled and go to the door.

'Who is it?' she whispers through the slats.

'It's Blom, Auntie.'

As she releases the latch, the wind blows open the door, and the hunched child rushes inside.

'Blom. What time is it? What are you doing here, *petite*?'

'Please, can Tannie come . . .?' Blom is out of breath. 'Please come. My mother is . . . my father, he hit my mother, and now my mother is lying on the floor and doesn't move.'

Camille takes a sharp breath. 'Okay. I'm coming. Wait for me, Blom. I'm coming now.' She tiptoes into the room where Pappi lies snoring, and takes his thick dressing gown from the end of his bed and puts it on. From the bathroom she throws into a plastic bag some antiseptic, bandages and the scissors Pappi very occasionally uses for trimming his beard.

'Let's go,' she says to Blom. Then, noticing how the

little girl is shaking, she grabs an old blanket lying on the chair. 'Here, wrap this round you. Quick. Let's go.'

How silent Blom is as she drags her along through the coarse grass, hedges and thickets in this starless, moonless night. The wind blows in powerful waves, wildly tossing about their clothes, the blanket, the plastic bag. The air smells of rain. Blom's hand grips hers very tightly. Through puddles, mud and sludge they make their way, snapping twigs underfoot and pushing branches away from their faces, until finally Camille finds herself in front of a row of tiny cottages, one or two still dimly lit with the cold blue light of paraffin lamps. The wind screams and somewhere in the distance a dog is barking. She shudders.

'Come. Tannie must come over here.' Blom pulls her to the end of the row, and pushes open the door. The room is silent. In the dark Camille picks up the sour smell of vomit.

'Have you a torch, or a candle, Blom?' She finds herself whispering, instinctively.

'Wait,' says Blom. 'I'll check by the stove.'

She hears Blom scuffling and swearing under her breath, an owl hooting through the wind. She pulls the nightgown tighter around her and refastens the cord. There is the sound of a match striking. Between Blom's tiny fingers the flickering light throws shadows in streaks across the room. And then Leah, collapsed open-mouthed in a small pool of blood on the floor.

Her first convulsive thought is that she must be dead. She drops onto her knees and, taking the wrist in her hand, finds her pulse with her fingers.

'Leah,' she says.

No response. A gash on her head still oozes blood.

'Blom. Go next door. We need help.'

75

Blom scuttles off. She can hear the knock, someone shouting 'Fokoff', the knock again and her little cry hollow and desperate: '*Asseblief!*'

Eventually, she drags a naked man from next door into the room.

'*Ja? Wat soek jy?*' he says.

'We need to get this woman to hospital.'

'*Ag, nee wat.* She'll be all right. She's always all right. *Daai's geen hospitaal hier nie*, my lady. Not for miles. And even then, is mos a white hospitaal. They's not interested in us there. Where's Goiya?'

'Who?'

'Goiya. Leah's husband. Seems he got a bit of a fright mos, and buggered off. Haai, must have given his missus one moerse klap this time. *Kyk hoe bloei sy. Foeitog.*' He whistles. 'It's the alcohol, my lady. Puts the devil in us mos.'

'What do you mean there's no hospital, no help? What about a doctor?'

'*Nee wat.* Nothing. A clinic on Tuesdays and Fridays. And they's not interested in our stories. Another klap from Oom Tas. So fokken what?'

'Well, would you help me carry her home?'

'Now?' he scratches his head. 'Where the hell is that?'

'There is never a convenient time to die, Mister. If we leave her here, she will die. Do you understand me? I do not live too far from the big house. Mr Smit's house.'

The man gives another long whistle and shakes his head in disapproval.

Blom stifles a little sob. '*Asseblief!*'

'What kind of man are you?' Camille says between her teeth.

'All right, keep your hair on. Let me just put some pants on mos. A man's got his decency, you know.' He leaves the room muttering, '*Dis mos 'n klap. Daai blerrie Goiya*. I'm gonna *klap* that bastard too. I'm gonna *moer* hom.'

While Camille and Blom wait for him to return, Camille bandages the wound on Leah's head. Blom holds a candle, fetches a little water from the tap, bends down close to her mother's face while Camille works. At the sting of the antiseptic, Leah jolts. For a second her eyes open, then again, before closing. In the streaky dimness, Camille cannot tell whether there is any flicker of recognition. Her eye falls on Leah's left arm, bent back at the elbow, broken like a toy doll. By the time the man next door returns, she has wrapped an extra sheet around the woman, binding her tightly, like an Egyptian mummy, and they prop her up between them, their arms around her waist.

'Show us the way, Blom,' she says. 'Little night fairy. Show us the way.'

By the time the first blades of light cut through the night's violent secrets and conspiracies, Leah has been laid on a makeshift bed of a few cushions and blankets. She has been cleaned and all her wounds are dressed. Camille has torn up an old pillowcase and with some elastic made a sling for her arm, which for now has been tightly bound; it will need to be set as soon as possible. Blom has collapsed in a small blanketed heap on the chair. Camille fires up the gas stove and boils some water.

As she sinks into the other chair, slowly sipping her tea, she feels something wet and warm at her ankles. Laika's nose and soft wet tongue. A moment later Zara crawls on to her lap, rubbing her eyes.

'Where were you?' she croaks.

'There was an accident. Blom's mother is hurt. And

Blom came all the way to find me in the middle of the night.'

As Zara slowly starts to focus, she realises that there are others in the room.

'Is that Blom in the blanket?'

'That's Blom, yes,' she strokes Zara's face. Then remembering the concert, lowers her voice. 'The night fairy.'

Zara stares first at her mother, then at the bundle on the chair alongside them, her black eyes stretching and widening as she silently absorbs this new piece of information.

The day unfolds in a peculiar peristalsis, the smallest events propelling it forward: Pappi waking and washing and coming to find out first where his dressing gown has gone, and then discovering what has happened. Blom waking and, somewhat quieter than usual, asking for something to eat. Camille getting Zara and Blom to help make a big breakfast; anything to distract them. And yet all their activities and conversations are quieter and more restrained than usual. Even the dog seems a little subdued. Although they avoid discussing it, each one of them is poised and waiting for Leah to move or to speak or to cry.

In a low voice, Camille relays the conversation about the hospital to her father.

'She needs to have her arm set, and soon. And she should be checked by a doctor.'

'Can you do it?'

'Set her arm?'

'Yes.'

'I could try, if I had some plaster of Paris. Don't you think she needs to see someone?'

'I think she is seeing someone. I think you are the best

78

one for the job. Particularly if the hospitals aren't helpful.'

She remembers the hospital where she worked in France. Assisting the doctors in resetting the broken bones of children who had come off their bicycles, old ladies who had lost their balance, men who fell off their motorbikes, or who drove their *vélocettes* too fast . . .

'I can do it,' she suddenly says with conviction. 'But perhaps I'll go up and speak to the Smits. They will need to know that Leah won't be coming to work for a while. I just don't want to go too far in case she wakes.'

'I'll watch her and the children. Go if you think you should.'

Camille closes the door behind her and squints in the sun. She rubs her burning eyes and tries to put some energy in her step. Halfway up the sweeping gravel driveway to their home, she realises that she has not even brushed her hair.

The driveway ends at a gargantuan front door, made from thick wood. A small red bicycle is propped up against a wall, handlebars falling disconsolately to one side. She lifts the thick brass knocker and lets it fall, hearing the bang reverberate through the high-ceilinged house. A while later a woman releases the door.

'Yes. Can I help you?' The woman has a clipped colonial accent. Her white blouse is stiffly starched.

'My name is Camille Pascal. I am your neighbour, in the cottage.'

'I know who you are.' She peers at Camille through gold-rimmed bifocals. 'Do come in.'

Camille follows her into the enormous quarry-tiled reception room, and into an equally large sitting room that smells of furniture polish. A Persian carpet sprawls across the length of the room. The sofa looks newly upholstered. Floral. A mahogany desk stands stiffly at an angle in the corner of the room. What appears to be a bar area opens up near the back of the room. From where she is sitting she can catch the glimpse and glint of a wall strewn with exotic knives.

'Please take a seat. I would offer you some tea, but I'm afraid our maid hasn't shown up today.'

'That's why I'm here,' says Camille.

'Oh. You know Leah?'

'In a way, yes. Her little girl is my daughter's friend.'

'I see.'

'There seems to have been some trouble. She's hurt. She has a bad cut on her forehead and I think she's broken her arm. I would like to get her to a doctor.'

'Oh, dear me,' Mrs Smit says slowly. 'She'll have to go to the clinic. There's a nurse there, twice a week or so, I'm not sure when it is.'

'I am a nurse. She needs a doctor.'

'Look, Mrs . . .'

'Camille. Camille Pascal.'

'Pascal. Let me put it to you this way. You are not from these parts. If you were, you would know that this kind of thing happens all the time. The Coloureds are a violent lot. And they drink far too much, which of course only makes it worse. If doctors were to get involved here, they'd be busy all the time. And the blighters would never pay them. It's really not worth their while; you can surely see their point. My advice to you? Stay out of it. They're a bad lot.' She rises from the overstuffed floral chair, as if to mark the end of the appointment.

Camille takes her cue, and stands up. Before she makes her way to the giant door, past the antique dresser with the china figurines, she says, 'I see. Thank you for your time. In the meantime, Leah will be away from work for a while.'

'Oh, I'm sure she'll be fine soon. You know the old saying: weeds don't die. As I say –' she gives a little laugh – 'this is hardly the first time this has happened, and it certainly won't be the last either.'

As the enormous door slams behind her, Camille exhales. Then, staring fixedly ahead, she crunches over the gravel and back into the long grass. As she turns the corner, just out of sight of the house, she hears the scuffle of feet, and a man clearing his throat.

'Hello,' he says. His skin is flushed, his small eyes darting to and from her face and body.

'Hello, Mr Smit.' She tries not to glare at him.

'Everything all right?' he asks, out of breath.

'Yes, thank you.'

'It's all okay? With the cottage, I mean? I see you fixed and painted the roof.'

'Yes, we like it very much.' She increases her pace, and then suddenly slows down.

'Actually . . .' She pulls at a long, curly strand of hair, and looking sideways at him through her lashes, smiles.

'What? A problem? Can I help?' Words spew from his mouth, from his crooked teeth, like spitty bullets.

'Well,' she sighs, then shakes her head. 'No, it's fine.'

'No, please, what is it? Anything I can do?'

'No, I don't think so.' She smiles.

'Try me. No harm asking.' She notices beads of perspiration breaking onto his forehead.

'I just wanted to let Mrs Smit, to let your wife know, that Leah won't be coming in for a while. It seems her husband beat her very badly.'

'Oh, ja,' he nods. 'Happens a lot.'

'It's a pity,' she turns her head slyly. 'It's such a pity

something isn't done to curb the alcoholism among the farm workers.'

'Ja, uh-huh,' he says, nodding quickly.

'I'm sure you agree?'

'Ah, ja. Ja. We're working on it.' He gives a quick smile, showing crooked, stained teeth, his face pink and shiny.

'I thought you would. It makes sense, doesn't it? I mean, if your workers are happy and healthy it means higher productivity, which is better for the employer. Surely?' She smiles. '*Au revoir*, Mr Smit.'

NINE

He arrives uncharacteristically early at the school. Even Trudy is not in yet. He paces in his office for half an hour, absent-mindedly checking timetables, and going over his notes for today's seminar. When the time finally comes for class to begin, he walks a little quicker than usual down the corridor, giving a brisk wave to Trudy, who has just arrived. Entering the room, he steals a glance at Zara's usual place at the back of the class. She is there. Sitting with head bent, matted hair falling across her cheek, working on some scrap paper with a piece of charcoal in her left hand while the other students talk among themselves. The tightness in his chest gives way.

Today's class follows a workshop format: he teaches a little, the students take notes, work through some exercises, before feedback and discussion. He is a little flushed. He forces himself to concentrate. He must be getting ill, he thinks. Or perhaps it is low blood sugar; no breakfast this morning. A fly keeps buzzing around the light.

He feels very aware of wanting to look at her, but resists. Now and again he casts a sidelong glance; she looks so peaceful. Or is it passive? Now and again her lips move, as though to whisper or say something. She seems to show no shame for scratching his face (she must see he still has the marks on his cheek). It's hard to believe that this is the same young woman who had torn at his face like a savage animal. In her world laminated by silence, mirrored in her void-filled eyes, she is the most isolated being he has ever come across.

Perhaps it is he who should apologise to her; for frightening her. But how? How could he explain to her that in that split second she had completely mesmerised him. It's ridiculous. Everything about this is quite ridiculous. Snap out of it, Jake, he tells himself. He can hear Maria echoing the phrase. Women may be powerful creatures, but this girl-woman – she must be what, eighteen? nineteen at most – is not even clean! He gives a little snort. Some students look up, exchange glances. She does not. Her head is still bent, her hand still sketching in long, smooth strokes.

How does he tell her that in that instant, seeing her curled up in the chair, he had been overcome by longing? That he had ached simply to touch her. To penetrate her silence. That he had drunk too much wine at lunchtime. It's unthinkable. Instinctively, he raises the back of his hand to his forehead, where small beads of perspiration are breaking. He must be ill. He should go home to bed.

The class discussion is brief and dry. He knows it is his fault; the class must sense his complete lack of animation and involvement. Only the relentless buzzing of the fly bridges the gaps of silence. He wishes he could scream. At the end of the period, the students file past him, dropping their exercises on his desk for marking. She walks with her head down. Then, as she leaves her contribution on his desk, she looks up at him. Anxious not to let her go, he says impulsively: 'Wait!'

She stops.

'Would you see me in my office some time, shall we say tomorrow morning?'

She nods. He continues, speaking a little quicker and a little softer than usual. 'Any time. Tomorrow is a prac day, so any time. I'll make sure I'm there this time.'

She nods again, then drops her head and walks away.

There is nothing in her face that gives him any clue to what she is thinking. No trace of anger or apprehension or joy. No smile, no frown. Her large black eyes are as remote as a night sky.

Trudy follows him down the corridor and into his office.

'Hello,' she says. 'You walked straight past me!'

'Did I? Sorry.' He sinks into his chair.

'No kiss?' She looks surprised.

'Kiss,' he repeats automatically. 'Kiss. Ah . . . kiss!' He conjures up a smile. 'You know I'm really not feeling well.'

'What's the matter?' She walks over to his side, and leans against his desk, a tiny suede miniskirt brushing the top of her tanned, toned thighs.

'Don't know.' He jumps up, moving to the window, looking out.

'What is it?' She runs her hand up his spine. 'Why so edgy? Can I help?'

'Just not feeling well.' He gives a thin smile. 'Actually, Trude, be a love and give me a few minutes, will you? I need to do some marking and then I think I'm going home.'

She stares at him for a few seconds. 'Okay. Suit yourself.'

'She closes the door, a little more firmly than usual, but he is too relieved to notice. As it clicks shut, he leans forward on to his desk and puts his head in his hands, spreading the perspiration across his forehead. Is this it then? Is this a breakdown? He stares across at the chair, now hers, where he found her curled asleep. Then picks up the pile of marking and his keys and heads for home.

When Maria returns from the gallery, he is still lying on his back staring at the ceiling, the pile of marking on the bed next to him.

'Rough day?' she asks, pulling off her shoes and flouncing onto the bed.

'Something like that.'

'What happened?'

'Nothing.'

'Hmm. Sounds stressful. What are these?' She toys with the pile of papers on the bed.

'Marking.'

Half absent-mindedly, she starts rifling through the pages. The private detective in her can never resist any raw material.

'Nice,' she says, stopping at one or two neat sketches. Then, 'This kid can draw.' She holds up a charcoal sketch of an owl clutching a rat. 'What did you use for a model for this?'

'Nothing. She does it herself.'

'She drew this from memory?'

'Yes. She does it all the time. Mostly when she's supposed to be drawing something else. It's bloody irritating.'

'What else does she draw?'

'Animals. Death. Violence in nature.'

'Hmmmm. Bit of a weirdo. But good, huh?'

'Most of my students are good at line drawing.'

'Come on, Jake.'

'What? They are.' She notices his voice is slightly higher than usual.

'This is not "most" students.'

'Please leave me alone, Maria. I have a headache and you're getting on my nerves.'

His cellphone buzzes. The discreet ring tone he has selected suddenly seems even more telling than the usual shrill alternatives. He clamps his jaw. Maria is watching him. The owl swooping in on the rat.

'Your phone,' she clips.

'I have a headache. I'm not answering. They can leave a message.'

'And you can disappear off to your car when you think I'm not looking and return the call.'

But he does not return the call. He forgets all about it. Not until the following morning, when Trudy knocks like a police officer at his office door and demands to know what has got into him, does he give it another thought.

'Close the door,' he says. 'Come now. Sit down.'

She flounces into a chair, crosses her legs, her neat little chin defiantly pointing upwards. He turns the key in the lock, just in case, before returning to where she is sitting. He wishes she had chosen the other chair. Not that chair. Trudy looks so different, so sophisticated in it. It doesn't suit her. He pats her on the leg, and returns to his desk.

'I'm not well, Trudy. Please try to understand.'

'What's the matter?'

'I wish I knew. I can't sleep. I can't paint. I'm forgetting things. And it's getting worse. Please don't be angry with me. I'm doing my best. You were always so supportive . . .' He allows his voice to trail away towards the faintest edges of reproach.

'I want to support you. I really do.' Her voice swells with emotion. 'It's just that I don't know how much longer I can go on like this, Jake.' She stares insistently at her foot, now tapping; an attempt to postpone the tears she knows are gathering force. He watches quietly, carefully. And then he rises from his seat, and kneels before her, taking her hand and stroking it.

'I understand. I really understand.' He looks down. Time enough to sharpen the knife: 'If you need to end it how could I blame you?'

'End it? No! Not end it. I'm not ready for that.' She gives a little laugh. 'Why, do you . . . ?'

'Of course not,' he whispers soothingly. 'You're the only good thing in my life.' He can see her chest relax a little and her spine loosen as she sits fractionally back in the seat. 'But I'm not well, Trude. I need to think about that. I can't be worrying about all the small things that may or may not be upsetting you. For your sake, for *our* sake, I need to work on my healing.'

He remembers the whispered plea, her legs still wrapped around him: *Please don't leave me*.

'I didn't realise,' she says quickly. 'I'm sorry, I really didn't realise, Jake, I haven't been supportive, I've been selfish, I'm so sorry.'

'That's okay. We all have our shadows. And you've always been so good at accommodating mine.'

'And now I haven't. Just when you most needed me. How awful!'

'Don't be so hard on yourself.'

'I'm just so glad we could talk. I feel so much better.'

'I'm glad too.'

'Thank you,' she whispers.

Someone tries the handle. Pushes against the locked door. Then knocks.

He jumps to his feet, knocking a book over. 'I have to see students. Can I call you later?'

'Yes, of course.' She quickly adds, 'But if you don't get round to it, I do understand. Be good to yourself, Jake.'

'Yes, I will.' His tone is brisk; an unconscious attempt to change the energy in the room. A light kiss on her cheek serves as the full stop punctuating the end of the interlude. Then he straightens up, turns the key and opens the door.

'Ah, Zara. Come inside.' His voice is jarringly jovial. He gives a cheery wave as Trudy moves into the passage. 'Thank you, Trudy. Bye.' Then turning to Zara he smiles politely, 'Come inside.'

As she brushes past him into his office, he inhales: yes, she smells like the rain. She settles herself into her chair. It must still be warm from Trudy. He takes his seat behind his desk.

'Look, uh, sorry about the other day. We seem to have got off on the wrong footing. I just wanted to explain some things to you. Now, I know you prefer to sketch and paint live models, and don't particularly like still life, but it's good exercise for you and part of the course anyway, and, yes.' He finds himself sucked into a vortex of words, his voice suddenly unnaturally high. He takes a quick gasp of air. She stares back at him. The inescapable gravitational pull of the black hole.

'Such black eyes,' he finds himself mumbling. 'You have very black eyes.' He tries a little laugh, as though he is making a joke. 'Not a colour, black is not a colour.'

'Black is all colours,' she says.

This voice, heard now for the first time, breaks into his composure. As though he has been caught in a sudden cloudburst. He stares back at her.

'I'm sorry, what did you say?'

She does not answer immediately. Then serenely, 'When you die your pupils take up your entire eye. You see everything when you die.'

Last night, when he had planned how he would deal with this situation, he had decided to take the avuncular approach; the 'I'm here to help' concerned teacher approach. But he suddenly feels stripped. Left standing naked in the rain. None of the roles he has played in his life has equipped him for this.

'I see. Sorry, you threw me a little there. You . . . you don't talk much, do you?'

She stares back at him. 'I paint.'

'Yes, I know. You have a very powerful style. Who taught you to paint?'

'My father.'

'Oh? What does he do?'

'He's dead.'

'Oh, I'm sorry. What did he do before he died?'

'He painted.'

'So you learned by example then. Often the best way.'

'I never met him.'

Impenetrable. Quite mad. So why, *why* is it so strong? This desire to possess her, to subdue her? To mark this uncharted territory irredeemably and irrevocably. To dig in the flag and conquer.

'Is your mother alive?'

'No. Is there anything else?' She leans forward to rise.

He wants to shout 'Stay!'

'No, that should be fine.'

His body feels like lead as he watches her dissolve into the student mass.

TEN

SHE IS WAITING at the window for her mother to return from the big house. She had wanted to go with her, but Maman said no. She had tried to follow but Pappi had called her back with elastic-band arms. And a man with a hat and a mouth like a mulberry had come to call for Leah, and Pappi had asked him to come back later. And Blom is asleep again. And Laika keeps thumping his tail. She blows vapour on the pane, and draws a swirl with her fingertip. Cold. And where is Maman? Has she had an accident on the way? Has a car come from nowhere and run her over? Is she lying somewhere? What will happen if she dies? *What if she dies?* What will happen to her and to Pappi and to Laika? She hears Leah moan and say something. She turns and sees Pappi taking her a glass of water with his big, slow steps. Blom is all curled up like a shell, and maybe she is a fairy and maybe she isn't, and how can she know unless Maman tells her for sure? She spins round to the window again. Is that her? Is that her maman coming down the pathway like she always does? Not dead, looking fine, no accident. Not even a smudge. Just fine, fine, fine.

'Maman!' She bangs on the window. Camille waves back. She has never quite understood why it is that Zara, usually so quiet, gets so excited, so abundantly relieved to see her, when she has been away only a few minutes. In this case only three-quarters of an hour at most. But already she knows that there will be a great reunion; all arms and legs and dog before silence and detachment return.

'How is she?' she asks Pappi while disentangling the child from her legs and lifting her on to her hip. 'Ah, Zara. You're getting so big to carry these days.'

'That's because I'm nearly six,' says Zara.

'She's awake. She had some water. The little one is asleep again,' her father answers.

She sets Zara on her own feet again and makes her way across to the makeshift bed where Leah is tentatively touching her head with her hand.

'How are you feeling?'

'S'fine.'

'You have a nasty cut on your head. And I think your arm may be broken. You should see a doctor.'

'S'fine.' She tries to lift herself from the bed, winces and drops back onto her good elbow.

'Then I'm going to have to try to set your arm myself.'

'Must go home,' she says. She hoists herself up once again.

'Please, at least let me look at your arm.'

She fetches some bandage and a couple of wooden spoons to use as splints and sets Leah's arm tight and neat. It hangs stiffly at her side, like a prop, inanimate.

Only then does she glance across at the blanketed heap, and realise that Blom has been watching them, wide-eyed.

'Good sleep?' asks Camille.

'Hullo, Mommy,' says Blom.

Camille disappears to wash her hands. When she returns, both Leah and Blom are gone.

'A man came looking for her,' Pappi says.

'Her husband?'

'Yes. I think so.'

'Now?'

'No, earlier, while you were up at the big house.'

'Did you give him a piece of your mind?'

'I was going to. But when I opened the door and saw him standing there like a bent stick, hat in his shaking hands, eyes pulled down with shame, his overalls hanging from him like an apology, I changed my mind. When a man is doing such a good job of punishing himself, it is best not to interfere.'

'Not interfere? He deserves to die for what he has done! Before he kills her.'

'Maybe death has come for him already. It's only the breathing that's still there.'

'You're too soft, Papa.'

'And you are hot-headed. You are not going to change this place single-handedly overnight. No matter how hard you want to.'

'I do want to.'

'I know. But it's going to take time, Camille. For your own sake and theirs, give it time.'

And then they start coming. First, one or two a week, then after a month, one or two a day. Henry Davids. Willie Solomons. Esmerelda Marais. Marietjie Philander. Those who have cut themselves on pruning shears and need a wound cleaned and bound. Those with colds and flu. Many of the women have bladder infections and need antibiotics. Many are pregnant and do not even know. Or do not want to know. She mixes her own remedies as far as possible. She is growing herbs in the garden especially for these purposes.

Spearmint and ginger for nausea. Potted marigold and chickweed for rashes. But for more acute problems, which is increasingly the case, she drives to Cape Town, to Groote Schuur Hospital, to get supplies.

But Mondays are the worst. Mondays are hangover days. Camille soon discovers that many labourers never show up to work on Mondays, ever. They are too busy sleeping it off, or throwing up, or shouting at their families and their God or somebody's mother's private parts. She also soon learns that by Monday it is all too evident which women have been beaten over the weekend.

'It's the ones that don't drink that fetch a klap,' one young Coloured woman tells her. 'They make trouble for the men: Where were you? Why didn't you come home? En so on. The men throw them with a klap. They don't like the woman to ask them questions they haven't got the answers for.'

'Like where is this week's wages and how am I supposed to feed the children?' says another woman, nursing a black eye.

'It's the alcohol, Miss Camille. The alcohol puts the devil in them.'

'And the blerry wine farmers don't help.'

'Why?' asks Camille.

'*Dopstelsel*. They pay the workers almost nooit. And what do they do to keep them quiet, and dronk and dependent? They give them wine, mos. Jugs and cans, full, every night. And more on the weekend.'

'Something must be done, Papa,' she says, slapping her hand on the table. If she could only do something, perhaps she could start making sense of her decision to come here.

'Something is being done. You're already making a difference.'

'But that's just symptomatic. Something must be done to change the system.'

'I agree with you, Camille. But it's tough. It seems to suit both parties.'

'Not the women,' she says.

'No, not the women.'

'And there's stories of children having foetal alcohol syndrome too.'

'Those that aren't heading for alcoholism themselves,' he agrees.

'I wonder if they even know the damage they are doing?'

'Who?'

'Both sides! The wine farmers for dishing it out. And the workers for taking it. Surely somebody, somewhere, agrees with us, Papa?'

'That I don't know. I wonder. There's a strange torpidness here. Local people seem to prefer to turn a blind eye.'

'Well, we are not local people!'

'Which is why they most likely won't listen to us.'

'We need to speak to the mayor, or the police. And the Smits, again. Mr Smit seems a little more reasonable than his wife. Perhaps if he knows what wine does to Leah's husband, he will help to protect her?'

'You can try, you seem to have some influence over him, but I don't hold out much hope.'

'I can try.'

'Camille?'

'Yes, Papa.'

'Don't hope too much. You don't want to be disappointed. This is a difficult country. We had no idea *how* difficult before we arrived. We are not going to change things overnight, if at all. Try to be content with what you have. And what you *are* doing. You have your hands full with Zara; she is such a sensitive child. And you are doing an excellent job. *Merveilleux.*'

'Thank you, Papa. But I want to be more useful. What else is there for me?'

The boy too comes almost every day now. Camille and Zara have learned to recognise the soft knock. The first time it happened, she opened the top half of the ranch door and looked out. Nobody.

'Hello,' the voice came from below.

'Pieter. I didn't see you.' His head was below door level.

'Does Zara want to ride my bike?'

How the two interact without Blom is difficult to say. Camille watches them in the garden playing – silent as flowers. When Blom does arrive, there is more noise. And sometimes tears. When Blom is not there, Pieter allows Zara to ride his bike. He even brings fairy wheels over at first, so that she can try it out without falling, his concern for her always touchingly fatherly.

On one occasion, Camille is spreading some sheets out to dry over a bush out the back when she finds Pieter kicking a stone with his veldskoen. His bike is propped up against the wall. He tries not to look at her as she pegs the edges of the sheets to a branch.

'What is it, *petit*?'

'Nothing.'

'Why are you not playing with the others?'

'Don't want to.'

'What a pity. It's such a lovely day not to play.'

'I don't like playing with Blom. She's unfair.'

'Unfair? Come here, hold these pegs for me while I do this.'

The little boy takes the container of pegs from her, still looking down.

'You know, *petit*, I want to tell you a secret. Would you like that?'

'Yes.'

She takes a peg from her mouth. 'Many times things are not fair. And it's hard! You want to say, "Wait! How can that be? I deserve better!" But you know, that's really not the point.'

He stares at her, his brows furrowed.

'The secret is . . .' She lowers her voice. Looks around. 'Do you want to know the secret?'

'Yes.'

'Are you sure?'

'Yes!'

'The secret is not whether anybody else is fair. But whether *you* are fair. That's all you have to worry about.'

'But I *am* fair. I play fair with Zara and Blom.'

'Then you have nothing to worry about, *n'est-ce pas*? Yes?'

He looks mistrustful.

'Now, come with me. We're going to have some juice, and see if we can find some Zoo biscuits. We'll soon see who gets called unfair.'

Much to Zara and Blom's surprise, he chooses to spend the rest of the afternoon with Camille, potting seedlings. Even when Zara comes quietly to his side and takes his hand and says, 'Come.'

'When I'm finished,' he says. 'I'm busy now.'

Camille has given him the job of taking the paper off some empty tomato tins. Together, they scoop up some soil and drop it in, before securing the fragrant seedlings with their fingers: sweet basil, mint and rosemary.

And then, a few weeks later, he stops coming. Blom is delighted. She talks faster than ever, her voice intermittently squeaking with pure joy as she speculates what is keeping him away.

'Fleas,' she says, nodding her head. 'Whole family got terrible fleas. My mommy says so.'

'Fleas! Are you sure, Blom?' Camille asks. She cannot imagine the Smits, with their immaculate home, even owning an animal. Certainly not one that would be allowed indoors.

'Ja, s'true. *Vreeslike vlooie*. Verry fierce fleas. Go *pienk, pienk, pienk*.

With every '*pienk*' she pinches Zara on the leg to indicate the jumping flea.

'Don't,' says Zara.

Blom squeals with laughter.

'*Pienk, pienk, pienk*.'

But it is only when Leah arrives to have her arm looked at again that they discover the truth.

'They beat him with a sjambok mos. Three times. And he doesn't cry.'

'Pieter? They beat their own son?'

'Three times. And he hold his mouth tight like this.' She tucks her lips in and pushes them together. 'But he don't cry.'

'But why?'

'I told you she's a funny one, that Mevrou Smit. Hard bitch, that's what. Thinks she's so fancy.' This is the most Camille has ever heard Leah say. Usually she is so contained. 'She say he must be punished, and make him fetch the sjambok for that fat *poephol* to klap him.'

'Leah, *why*?'

'Because he come here.'

'Here? You mean to play?'

'Ja, here. She say . . . she say, now wait a minute, lemme say it exactly like her.' In an affected tone she says: "I've told you before, Pieter, not to mingle with *those* people. They behave like gypsies. Vagrants. And they're *dirty*!" And then the *poephol*, all pink and sweating by his armpits, klaps him.'

Camille resets Leah's arm in silence. She struggles to adjust to Leah's change in behaviour. This usually reserved woman, now so animated with anger. Could it be that she felt they were all now reduced to the same level? Co-victims. Less than. Insulted. Or is it because she knows Camille may well have saved her life?

With Mrs Smit's opinion she does not concern herself. It is, after all, only her opinion. But the treatment of the boy is appalling. That serious, unhappy little boy means no harm. And she knows that Zara really likes him. It also now means that the Smits are beyond the pale in terms of trying to change the *dopstelsel*.

As Blom disappears with her mother, Zara goes to the door to look out.

'Pieter won't be coming today, *petite*.'

'Did they really hit him?' Her eyes seem old and grave. She must have overheard then.

'That's what Leah says. Yes. His father hit him.'

Zara nods, then falls silent. A while later she looks up. 'No fleas then.'

'No fleas.'

'What's a sjambok?'

'I don't know. I don't think I want to know either. Come, let's take Laika for a walk. Let's walk to the dam, it will make us feel better.'

She takes her daughter's hand and they fall into the

silent rhythms of walking. As they thread their way along the paths that lead to the dam, they walk past a field of vines. A barbed-wire fence separates them from the Smits' vineyard, but the two will not look sideways. Were they to do so, they may catch sight of an overweight man with a ruddy face who stops and watches them pass. They may see him put down his belongings and follow them, keeping a little way behind, until they reach the dam. But they do not. Instead, Zara lifts her dress over her head and climbs out of her knickers. And Camille loosens and removes her skirt, keeping only her T-shirt and underwear on. She sinks into the cool water and closes her eyes, imagining that the water is cleansing them from sin.

ELEVEN

AND THEN MARIA starts showing up at the school. She sails past Trudy with a disparaging glare – a 'don't even *try* to stop me' look – and flounces into Jake's office. She doesn't know anything for sure. But she has her hunches.

'What are you doing here?'

'Nothing in particular. Just wanted to say hello.'

'I see. How nice.'

On one occasion, after waiting an annoying amount of time in his office, she eventually slides into the back of a classroom. To observe.

She sees Jake look at her briefly, unflinching, and continue with his lecture. History. Sculpture. Rodin.

'While Rodin was never considered good enough to be admitted into the prestigious École des Beaux-Arts, he was a graduate of the National School of Decorative Arts. By the time he was forty-three he had a marketable skill: he was able to keep himself alive doing decorative pieces and working as an assistant to several sculptors. He also knew some well-connected Parisians, and had been welcomed into artistic, literary and political society. Let's face it, Rodin knew only too well about what today we would call "networking" and the politics of self-promotion. He managed to do portrait busts of many influential men, including Victor Hugo, and thus link his name with theirs.'

She leans forward, elbows on the desk, chin on her hands. She has always enjoyed Jake's mind. His ability to pick out details that bring his subject matter home. It's been so long since they've had a decent discussion about anything. Jake seems to save his brain for others, or the media, or crowds or groups of people like this. She scans the class. Are they listening?

Art students: the avant-garde, the pierced, those with oxygenated hair, others with oxygenated brains. Leather, studs, crocheted multicoloured skirts. Black. Orange. Acid green. North African garb. Her eye falls on a tall girl at the back of the class. Greasy hair, shapeless clothes. Mind seems to be elsewhere. Is she doodling with that pencil, or drawing? She's not listening to Jake, that's for sure.

Even though some of them seem to go out of their way to make themselves as unattractive as possible, she admires the careless beauty of the young. The boys with their long shorts and sunglasses inhabiting their bodies with exaggerated pride. The girls, young women really, smooth and firm and unsure, flirting with their own charm. It must be the wisdom of the gods to infuse most women with rare glimpses of their own power only once they are past this age, with its potent force of nubile volatility.

At that age she had completed an expensive cookery course at one of the finest schools in the country and was heading for London for a gap year with some old school friends. They were all over-eager and under-experienced, with too strong a 'safety net' in the form of parentally enthused subsidies ever to fret much about anything. They hadn't a clue what they wanted to do with their lives, but they were determined to find out.

In search of 'culture' she had spent weekends

traipsing through art galleries and exhibition halls. She loved the feeling of awe that permeated their spaces like an invisible fog. A dense silence. There was something transcendent about art. It was the domain of the gods. From the perfection of the classics she started a tentative investigation into modern art. A realm of quirkier gods. Each painting a secret, evanescent. A code of colour and texture that kept its core cohesion from her. What did it *mean*? How to unlock it? Who was the key?

She treasured these questions. On her return, she considered them of far greater value than any of the souvenirs and bad photographs taken by intoxicated friends at parties. It was questions like these, she felt, that shape a life. That act as signposts on the journey. She had enrolled at university to study art appreciation, but had not completed the course. A wealthy boyfriend talked her into the far more practical world of art buying, selling, importing and exporting. Her family hoped they would marry – his family were sugar barons like themselves – and instead of persuading her to continue her studies, encouraged her to follow him into the business. By the time he left her for a model, she was starting to develop a name for herself in the import/export industry, and decided to prove to herself and everyone else that she could make it on her own. And she did. She smiles to herself. Nobody saw or knew what it cost her. Thank God.

But in the end, her job was more about catching aeroplanes, sleeping in strange hotels, selling and administration than it was about art. She remembers it well. Endless runways. Remembers realising that she still had questions to unlock. Artists to discover. And then, of course, she met Jake, who instantly became not only the key, but the creator.

That was ten years ago. She was thirty-five and slim. A novice in the art world trying to learn as much as she could. And trying to convince people that she knew her 'stuff'. Her parents lent her the money to buy the gallery in Constantia. Tucked between the popular coffee shop and a travel agency that promoted exotic holidays to Machu Picchu and fabulous round-the-world cruises, she felt she couldn't go wrong. She persuaded them it was an investment. In herself, in the perpetuation of artistic talent, in the future of art in this country. She was buying stock, selling too, and suddenly found herself the recipient of dozens of invitations to exhibition openings and lunches. Artists were paying attention to her. She liked it.

She met him at an opening of a sculpture exhibition. He too was trimmer then. And a little scruffy if truth be told. Boyish, with haphazard hair and warm blue eyes. Eyes that could slice through you too. Eyes that blazed and sharpened. He had walked over to her with a cut-glass champagne flute, handed it to her and said: 'I'm Jake Coleman. Who are you?'

At thirty-six Jake had earned himself a decent reputation in certain circles. But what he needed was a dynamite campaign to catapult him to the stars. She couldn't think of anyone better suited for the job.

'Maria Golding. I've heard of you.'

He smiled. And later came home with her.

And that was ten years ago. Jake had dazzled her. Amused her. Fascinated her. She loved to watch the creative process in action. The growing pensiveness, a swelling and breaking of ideas, then the quick sketch, sometimes in the middle of the night, and ultimately the hours of focused intent in the studio. A new painting born.

'You have a fabulous voice,' she remembers whispering as he lay alongside her that first night.

But he did not hear her, already snoring softly towards his future. She lay watching him for some time. The tousled hair. Eyelids soft as a baby. The patchy stubble around the chin. The slightly cruel mouth that looked as if it had been cut in one quick knife stroke.

For a long time they could hardly keep their hands off each other. A force like greed seemed to bound between them like an unstoppable child. There was no mood that could not be expressed in bed. Joy, sadness, even anger were simply the background music for what she always believed flowed deeper. She smiles ruefully, thinking only indifference finds nothing to celebrate at the banquet of pleasure.

And now the endless slippery grapple to get back to that euphoric launch platform where all that is new and eternal is the opiate for any uncomfortable reality. Where the fuel of hormones, the frisson, propels each to believe that the other is the vital ingredient. The fear that without it, the magic expired, there would be only her left. Exposed. Insufficient.

She cannot remember when the suspicions began. Perhaps they had always been there, masked at the start by passion-induced inviolability. The silent shadow in the pause of every conversation. An ever-present subterranean question.

Jake has always noticed women. At first, she convinced and consoled herself that his appreciation was not only natural, but honest. But there are times when she feels diminished. Times when walking with her he will spin right round to stare at a passing beauty. The split-second connection with another. Who is she in that moment?

She busies herself reading popular books on psychology and spirituality. Endless case studies of those who have loved – and won! – thanks to a philosophy or an epiphany or an affirmation repeated often enough. She attends wellness workshops, goes to yoga on the days when she doesn't have aerobics. Tries to understand the Kama Sutra. She has learned about wardrobe planning, aromatherapy, detoxing and colonic irrigation. Magazine articles, astrology, numerology, the Tarot. She has tried them all. But still it remains a mystery; that ineluctable 'principle' that will change everything. Make her good enough.

He is winding down his lecture. Some of the students have their hands up for questions.

'Wasn't one of Rodin's lovers a sculptor?' a boy asks.

'Camille Claudel. Yes. A very good one. It's a tragic story.'

'Do people think she may have been better than him?' the boy asks again.

'Only those that don't know,' he answers.

She examines each one closely again. How sad that she can no longer appreciate another woman's loveliness or talent without immediately feeling threatened by it. What happened to her big-heartedness? Has her spirit been so corroded that every woman becomes a danger? It is a compulsion. She cannot help herself, even now. Each young female here scrutinised. But no, she finally concludes. None of the students, young and nubile as they may be, seems to be Jake's 'type'. But that waspish secretary in the tiny skirt, she's bad news.

Jake is very polite to her on these visits. But not warm. She will need to find a way to validate her reason for visiting.

'So,' she says, playing for time.

'What?'

'I was thinking.'

'Yes?'

'What about an exhibition for your students at the gallery?'

'Think so?'

'Why not? It would give them something to work towards. And a fresh slant for the gallery.'

'It's very non-you.'

'I don't agree. I'm all for new ideas for the gallery.'

'Not when it involves amateurs.'

'I know. I have to be careful. But this is a bit different.'

'How so?'

'Well, let's see. It can be positioned as supporting the youth, the artists of tomorrow, that kind of thing. We can give the school a good punt too.'

'It doesn't need a "good punt", Maria. We have a waiting list.'

'Well, then we can make sure it gets longer!'

'Let me think about it.'

She looks large and out of place here. He cannot put his finger on it. Too old? Too overdressed? Too bejewelled? He wishes she would leave.

The following morning he tries to walk past the school office without being speared by one of Trudy's sullen stares. Since Maria has started sweeping in unannounced, she has grown very quiet, and he suspects very angry. But he cannot think about that now. He cannot worry about everybody. Not when he himself is struggling so.

He shuffles into the lecture theatre, absorbing the chatter of students as he walks towards the lectern. He swings around and faces the students. She is not there. Maybe late. He shuffles his papers, looks at his watch. Give it another minute. And then another minute. *What if she doesn't come back?* After ten minutes, the class growing steadily noisier, he begins, glancing across at the doorway at each pause. But she does not arrive.

The next day is no different. She is absent.

Later, in his office, he attempts marking essays. He feels intolerably hot. Jumps up and opens a window, standing there for a moment as the stiff breeze cools his face. *What if she doesn't come back?* The low buzzing of the computer in the far corner of his desk suddenly seems very loud. He reaches across and switches it off, feeling himself start to tremble. His heartbeat steps up. He takes a deep breath, but his breath seems stuck somewhere in his throat. He cannot get it any further down. He must be having a heart attack. Or losing his mind. Or both. He picks up the black telephone and dials the front office.

'Trudy, come here quickly.'

'What?'

'Quickly, goddammit! I'm in trouble. I need to get to hospital.'

'What you have described is an anxiety attack,' says the doctor.

'A what?'

'A panic attack. I'll prescribe some low-dose Valium for you, to take when you feel you need to take the edge off. But otherwise you may want to think about taking a break sometime.'

He is silent in the car on the way back to the school. It was not a heart attack. Nor is he losing his mind. Not yet. Only as they drive in does he turn to Trudy and speak.

'Trudy, I need you to find the contact details of one of the students.'

'Sure. Which one?'

'Zara. Pascal.'

'The grubby one? Why?'

'She's been away, and I need to get hold of her. For an exhibition.'

'Fine. Are you sure you're okay now, baby?'

'Quite sure, thanks.'

There is no phone number. No e-mail. Only a physical address. He might have guessed; she lives in one of the valleys, some distance away. When she has not appeared for over a week, he takes an afternoon off and drives into the valley. It is always like that; you drive for ever on tarred roads through varied vegetation and wealth, turn to navigate a mountain pass, and round the next bend, like a precious jewel held with both hands, the fertile valleys of the Cape. Stopping at the petrol station, he asks for directions. He is pointed to the local store: a dusty shop filled with bric-a-brac, brass, odd tables and chairs. Among the paraphernalia his eye passes over some decrepit pieces of wooden furniture, mahogany, teak, which would need only the smallest bit of attention to be transformed.

'Like a drink?' the owner asks. An overhead fan wobbles and whirrs, making a clicking ticking sound with each revolution. From an old gramophone comes the croon of the saxophone. Some honky-tonk.

'No, thanks. I'm looking for the home of the Pascal family. Do you know where I can find them?'

'Pascal? The crazy ones? They live over there, off the wine farm Three Oaks. Just take the dust road, and turn left at the sign that says Smit and then left again. It's a rondavel. Tin roof.'

'Thank you.' Jake is about to leave when suddenly he turns.

'Excuse me. Why do you call them "the crazy ones"?'

'Everybody calls them that.' He taps his temple vigorously with the tip of his index finger. 'They're mad, that girl and her grandfather. *Bossies*. But at least they keep to themselves these days.'

'What do you mean?'

'Girl's mother was a bit of a busybody. Good-looking, mind you. But she made trouble for herself. It was a nasty business. Ah, look who's here! Good morning, Tertius.'

Another customer has grabbed his attention – a regular by the looks of it. A cup of muddy coffee is immediately produced and the two sit squarely down, their elbows propped on a dusty table.

He drives slowly away from the store, repeating the instructions in his head: wine farm, dust road, Smit, rondavel. Crazy people. He called them crazy people. Something must have happened. *Wine farm, dust road, sign, sign*. Ah, he peers through the dust at a dark green board with the words 'Three Oaks' written on it. Beneath it, the customary family name; in this case, yes: 'Smit'. He turns down into the road that leads to the farm. After a while he sees another road veer left into what appears to be a thicket of trees, wild flowers and brush. His BMW does not have a high chassis, and now and then scrapes and bangs the dirt and stones beneath it. He drives past what must be labourers' lodgings, where cracks bite into loose plaster walls and wide pavements of dust are broken by only the occasional splash of colour – wild cannas, red and orange. Tin roofs are held in place by branches, stones and even the occasional pumpkin. Now and again a dog on a rope. Old lace inside a kitchen window. He pulls over to one side for a sky-blue tractor with a brick-red trailer, carrying bales of hay like shredded wheat. Eventually, he reaches a rondavel with a tin roof. A dirty old Citroën, cream-coloured, like a helmet, stands beneath an old oak tree. He stops alongside it and switches the engine off. Then takes a deep breath, opens the car door and gets out.

It is silent. So accustomed is he to the hum of the suburbs and the endless bustle of restless Cape winds that he feels self-conscious in this vast stillness. Exposed. He scratches under his chin and makes his way to the front door. He knocks and clears his throat. It strikes him that he has not planned what he is going to say. *What is he doing here? It's not as though he even knows!*

When the door remains unanswered he wanders around to the back. Finding the back door open, he sticks his head inside what must be the kitchen. The old man with the long white beard stands like a genie in a pink-and-yellow checked shirt, his jeans held up by lime-green braces, his back to the door, washing potatoes at the sink. To Jake, he seems thinner than the previous time at the art school. Jake clears his throat. No reaction. He must be deaf. That must be why he did not listen when he visited the school. He clears it again.

Whether he is deaf or not is unclear. After a while he turns round and without so much as a flinch points out through the window. In a voice dry as dust, he says, 'Over there. Walk on the pathway till you start to hear water.' He pauses to wait for air, then takes another breath. 'Climb up a level and wait for a dog to bark. Follow the barking and you will find her.'

Jake stares at him. 'I see,' he says. 'Thank you.'

He finds her under a tree sitting on a fallen log, a sketchpad on her lap, a handful of stubby chalk pastels, oily paper peeling from them, at her feet. She does not look up. He stands some paces away, the distance one might keep when admiring a sculpture, his head tilted to one side, watching. A dog flops at her feet, lifting its head now and then to give the odd bark; a reprimand. Still she does not look up.

'Hello,' he says.

She continues drawing, occasionally bending to consider another colour, her hair falling in a dark tangle before her face. She examines the pastel in her hand, then changes her mind and picks up another. Her hands are smudged with colour. There is something, crayon or pastel or dirt, wedged beneath her nails. He scratches the back of his head and clears his throat.

After a while she stops, rests the pastel on the drawing and looks up. 'Wild daisies,' she says. 'Orange and yellow. Did you see them on your way up the path?'

He blinks and swallows. 'Yes.' He feels as though he has been given the password. Allowed entrance to a world beyond. He knows now, he does not know how, that he need not explain why he is here. It is as if she has always known he would come.

He takes a step forward to peer at the picture. 'What are you working on?'

The dog growls without lifting his head. He takes another step forward. The dog growls again, his eyes swivelling to white to follow the intruder without moving his head.

Then he is behind her, looking over her shoulder at her picture, large and bold, of a baboon whose brains are exposed. From his cranium spreading outward like a halo are lightning bolts. From the lightning bolts are little drops, red like blood dripping. And a wolf howling at the moon.

'You draw like that without a model?' he voices.

'I have a model.'

'Where?'

'My dreams.'

'A baboon with lightning from his brains?'

'I often dream of baboons. And wolves.'

He walks around her and the dog and seats himself on a large rock near her, aware of the crackle his polished Italian shoes make on the twigs and bracken. The faint sound of water in the background.

'And blood. There's always blood in your pictures. Why?'

'Because that is how I see it.'

'See what?'

'My dreams.'

She sets the drawing down alongside her, then folds her stained hands on her lap and faces him.

'Are you scared of blood?' she asks evenly.

'No. Of course not. It's just a little . . . sinister, that's all.'

'Blood? Do you think so? That's interesting.'

'Why is it interesting?' He starts to smile. He wants to wrap himself around her and absorb her. To encapsulate her 'otherness' and own it. He wants to kneel before her and place his head in her lap.

'That you should think of it as something dirty,' she says.

'Not dirty. Just sinister.'

She looks away. In her black eyes the sky is mirrored. Then turns to him again; now it is his reflection that he

113

sees. 'It is blood that moves the heart. It is blood that moves the hand to draw. Blood is about life. And love. Not about death.'

'How did your mother die?' he asks.

'I don't remember.'

She rises from the broken log and walks towards him. The dog stands too and shakes himself out. She takes his hand. 'Would you like to see the waterfall?'

He walks with her as obediently as the dog. Their shoulders are the same height, brushing. She guides him along the path, then pulls him up to a flat area, a mangle of trees and rocks. They follow the pathway, dipping under the thorny branches till they reach a small pool of water, surrounded by rocks, green and foaming with moss and algae. Within the mud and rock enclave, a waterfall, clear and spumescent, cascades forcefully down one side. She releases his hand. 'Swim?'

What surprises him most is that he is not surprised. Here in this other country, this land inhabited by one, where he has been allowed a visitor's permit for this time, and maybe this time only, he watches the customs with awe and fascination.

'Not just yet. You go ahead.'

'There. That's a good rock for sitting.' She points to a large, dry ochre mass on the other side of the pool. He makes his way over and, in spite of its size, wrestles with it a little to test for firmness. By the time he sits down she has removed her clothes, and is sliding naked into the pool. In one smooth underwater stroke she emerges on his side. For a moment she lies back and floats, light and water snaking and blinking over her skin. Then lifts herself half out the water, her hair – that grimy hair – pulled black and sleek away from her face. It hangs down like a wet leaf, covering her breast on one side, but not quite on the other, exposing its contours and shadows, the dark nipple hard and puckering with cold. With her eyes closed and her face pointed upward, he realises that this is the closest he has come to seeing her smile. He leans forward instinctively, his hands outstretched, the way one might try to win the confidence of a wild animal. 'Come,' he says above the drama of the waterfall, slowly rising. 'Come to me.'

She rises out of the pool, fluid and liquid as a fish, the water coursing down her back and her front and her thighs, gleaming like scales as it catches the broken light.

She is as tall as he. He does not have to bend as she leans forward to kiss him, softly, lightly at first. Then with the full force of her power, she bites his bottom lip as hard as she can. Blood spurts hot and salty into his mouth and down his chin. In her blank eyes he sees the reflection of a man crying out in anger and pain, before they close and crinkle into the gurgle of a girlish laugh.

'To love is to bleed,' she says. Then sinks back into the pool and swims away.

TWELVE

AFTER A WEEK of tending the ailments and listening to the complaints of the workers in the area, Camille asks about the clinic that is available to workers twice a week.

'It's two hours twice a week. Tuesdays and Fridays. Sometimes we can't time our accidents so good to fit in with them,' says Willie Solomons.

'They treat us like children mos, Miss Camille. Like we're naughty boys and girls,' says Marietjie Philander. 'Always a big sigh and shaking their big heads.'

'I think it's time I went across and introduced myself,' she says. 'Maybe I can help, who knows.' A little seed of hope. Perhaps a fresh start. If they could only get to know her a little better, maybe they would accept her one day too. And allow her to be part of the healing process.

She gives it a few days' thought. After her unsuccessful visit to the Smits, she can only deduce that simply walking in to 'talk' to people does not work here. She must think it through carefully before she introduces herself at the clinic. She must not offend them. She takes a long look at herself in the small piece of mirror in the bathroom. She does not look like the people who live here. Perhaps it is this that offends them. She does not perm her hair, nor set it in rollers, and her clothes are not always functional or sensible. She is definitely thinner than most of the women here too. There are two types of people, she believes: those who are stimulated by difference, and those who find it threatening. Where she comes from, it is mostly the former; where she lives now, she suspects it is the latter that divides and isolates. A few days later she takes the Citroën through the pass, to the town on the other side of the mountain, where there is a women's clothing store. After examining each item in the store, and even trying one dress on, she leaves heavy-hearted and empty-handed, except for a pair of sensible court shoes. To buy drab, badly cut clothing simply to be accepted suddenly seems absurd. But perhaps her strappy high heels are inappropriate for first impressions.

On the Friday she wakes early to wash her hair so that she will have time to dry it in the sun before tying it back with a bright scarf. She chooses a French print dress, navy and white, with simple lines, and digs around for an old compact of compressed powder. Finally the shoes. Zara watches every move.

'Are you going to wear *those* shoes?' she asks.

'Yes.'

'Why?'

'Well, I don't know. I thought I should get some decent shoes. Why? What's wrong with them?'

'They're *brown*!'

'They're not brown, they're beige. It's a good colour with all this dust.'

But Zara's face speaks pure contempt as she glares at the shoes.

Her eyes follow her mother as Camille lifts a leather suitcase from the top of the cupboard, drops it on to the crumpled bed and unclips it. Inside, there are two things: an old concertina file and a bundle of papers in a pumpkin-coloured folder, tied with a piece of string.

'What's that?' Zara points to the orange folder.

'Oh, just letters. Nothing really.'

'What do they say?'

'Nothing. Really,' she repeats. She is flustered, rifling through the concertina file. Finally, she pulls out some papers, a little wavy at the edges, and smiles. 'Ah, here they are. My nursing qualification and some references. They're in French, but still.' She places the papers carefully in a bag, closes the suitcase and snaps it shut.

'Can I come too?'

'Stay with Pappi, Zara. Okay? Maman has to speak to some people and it will be boring. When I get back we'll go swimming.'

'Then will you take those shoes off?'

'Yes.'

'Will you be away for a long time?'

'No, of course not. I'll be back soon. Look after Pappi and Laika for me.'

Zara stares back at her, her black eyes large and luminous.

She watches her mother leave, then takes her place at the window until she sees her grow smaller and smaller, no bigger than a crayon, in the distance. Pappi is sitting at the table pretending to be reading the newspaper, but really he is finding out about the horses and making notes in the margin. She trots back to the big leather suitcase lying on their bed, and the pumpkin folder with the string. With both hands she presses on the rusty clips, first one then the other, until they pop open. The pumpkin folder is smooth and a little faded in parts, and the string is tied in a double bow. She fiddles with it for some time, her tiny fingers trying to prise it loose, but her nails are either too short, or too soft, and she cannot get a grip. '*Fok*,' she mutters. Finally, she hops off the bed and walks to the kitchen drawer where she knows she will find a pair of scissors with chipped red handles.

'Everything okay, *petite*?' Pappi asks without looking up from his sums.

'Yes. Just need a scissors.'

'Be careful.' He is peering through his glasses as though they are very far down his nose, and using a soft pencil with an eraser at the top.

'I know.'

She hops back on to the bed and snips the string. The folder releases its contents; several pages with blue writing. She wishes she could read. She knows how to write her own name. And Maman's. She can see her maman's name, 'Camille', now and again. But nowhere does she read her own name. The writing is pretty with its long strokes and letters with tails. She lifts the pages to her face; paper smells like Pappi's pipe.

'Zara?' Pappi calls. 'Come. Let's make tea.'

She drops the letters, scattered about like dry leaves, on the bed.

The clinic is in prefabricated rooms behind the post office. The black wrought-iron security gate is open. Inside, the floors are grey cement and people sit on two long rows of hard benches. On the walls are posters in red and white promoting family planning. There is a resigned placidity. Camille takes her place on the bench, and waits. She sees two nurses enter and exit the second room. The first, a middle-aged woman, short and efficient. The second, a young colt of a girl, smiling and anxious to help. The two appear to work together. One by one, at irregular intervals, the patients stand up and follow them meekly into the second room, emerging with packets of pills, or clutching the place where a needle has punctured their skin.

At the end of the two-hour shift, there are still four people and Camille waiting to be seen. The short nurse with the short hair looks down at the watch hanging like a claw from her pale green uniform and announces that they are now closed.

'What about us?' Camille turns to ask a young woman sitting next to her with a sick baby.

'Tough luck. Better show up earlier next time,' the young woman replies with a sigh, before picking up her bag and swinging her baby on to her hip.

'Wait,' Camille whispers. 'Your baby is sick. It shouldn't have to wait till Tuesday. Come and see me. I'm a nurse. I may be able to help.' She scribbles directions on a piece of scrap paper before walking across to the nurses, now packing their things to leave. She holds out her hand to the older woman in the flat black lace-up shoes.

'Hello. I've come to introduce myself. I am Camille Pascal.'

The woman gives her hand a curt shake. 'Yes, hello. We're closed now. You'll have to come back.'

'No, you don't understand. I'm not sick, I'm –'

'Then why are you here, lady? Can't you see how busy we are?'

'I'm a nurse,' she finishes emphatically.

'Then you can treat yourself, can't you?'

'No. Well, yes, of course I can. I don't mean that. I'm here to find out if I can help, that's all. I'd like to help.'

'There's no helping these people. They never learn. Live by the bottle, die by the bottle. There's no helping them.' The younger girl, her benign smile fixed, nods her head in agreement like a toy dog with its head on a spring.

'But couldn't you use an extra pair of hands here? You seem understaffed. I have my papers. My certificates. My qualification.' She holds them out.

'We're fine, lady. Just fine. And we're closed now, so if you'll s'cuse me.'

Camille stares at them in disbelief. 'Yes, you are closed. Very closed. I can't believe it.'

'Yes, yes, we know, we know,' the squat one says while ushering her out through the door. 'Goodbye.'

When she arrives home, the young woman with the baby is already waiting for her.

'I's on my way home but the baby, she's getting hotter and hotter.'

Camille drops her bag on the stoep and takes the child from her. Her eyes grow wide.

'Papa! Zara! Run the bath full of cold water. Quickly!' She turns to the mother. 'She's lost consciousness. It's probably the temperature.'

She lowers the child into the cold water. A few seconds later the tiny creature begins to cry.

'Oh, thank God,' says Camille. 'Now for some medicine.'

The baby takes the liquid in its purple-rose mouth, coughs it up and cries. The whites of her crinkly eyes are veined red with fever, her soft curly eyelashes wet and gluey.

'We need to get her to hospital, ' Camille tells the young mother.

'What's wrong with her?'

'I don't know. But we need to go now.'

'There's no hospital here in the valley.'

'We're going to have to go to Cape Town, to the Red Cross.'

The old man is already rummaging among the newspapers, searching for the car keys to give to her. 'I'll come with you,' he offers. He knows how fast she can drive if she is angry.

The baby has meningitis. It must stay at the Red Cross for thirteen days.

'You wonder how many die, simply because there's insufficient care,' says Camille in the car on their way home. 'What would have happened to that baby had I not met that young woman today?'

Her father sucks on his pipe and nods. 'Who knows?'

'Or cares.' She is angry. What is wrong with this place that complacent arrogance is allowed to cost lives?

'You know, Papa,' she thinks aloud, 'it's coming down to this: either we do something to help, to change this situation. Or we must go home.'

'To France?'

'Yes.'

'Ah, Camille! But you were so sure you didn't want to be there. You wanted a fresh start. A new life. You have to stop running away sometime, Camille.'

She bites her lip.

'Anyway, I think we did the right thing coming here. Don't you remember, I had just won on number thirteen – Lily Marlene, thirty-five to one – nobody could believe it. That was a sign if ever we needed one, yes?'

She smiles. 'You and your number thirteen.'

'She was number thirteen in the thirteenth race. Without her we wouldn't have been able to afford to up and leave!'

'You mean run away.'

'Well, we're not running now, are we?' he says evenly. 'Because now there is the child to consider.'

'I know,' she sighs. 'And anyway, this is the end of the earth. There is nowhere else to go.'

My love, how hard it is for me to write this letter . . .

Memory is the blade of a knife. How quickly you can collapse a life into a few suitcases when the need is there. At the time she did not ask herself too many questions; it was that very thing she needed to excise: the need to ask why. She looks across at Papa in the passenger seat, his newspaper open on his lap, plotting his racing permutations. He too knew not to ask too many questions. Knew full well that if he had not agreed with her at the time, she would have gone on alone. The drive to protect her as strong as his own fears of loss and loneliness.

Where to go? The ends of the earth. The very tip of Africa. On a whim! It was irresponsible. Papa is right. And just because Juergen had come here for a wine-making conference and fallen in love with the place. Had written to her of dramatic land and seascapes. Of mountains that were pink and blue, depending on the season and the setting sun. She had also heard that there were little pockets of the Cape that the French Huguenots had loved and marked with the flavour of France. She imagined a place where it might be similar enough to feel the edge of belonging, yet different enough to assure her that she was far enough away. The end of the earth. Oceans and continents and cultures to cushion her. A place where one can be forgotten. A place where one can forget. Juergen's letter had arrived soon after the other one . . . At the time, she took it as a sign. The place he described, the Cape, South Africa, sounded magical enough to bring a broken heart. And she vowed she would not return to France until it had healed.

And it is beautiful, the landscape, God, it is beautiful. She remembers the day they drove over the pass and down into the winelands for the first time. It was almost spring. Beyond the acid-lime canola fields a thousand variations of green. The cool afternoon sun washing over graveyards of peach and plum trees, their filigree skeletons pink and glowing, while bruised mountains held the community, with its lush farms, metallic blue dams and neat little row of shops in its arms. She remembers taking off her sunglasses and thinking, *Yes! This can be home*.

She turns to the old man, her eyes fiery. 'I'm going to start my own clinic. I'm going to speak to the hospitals, see if I can obtain some state-sponsored supplies. Come, Papa, what do I have to lose?'

'Keep your eyes on the road, Camille,' he says softly. More than that he cannot answer. He knows that her passion and her great heart will always be her salvation, and that on the other side of the same coin, if she is not careful, her reckless impulsiveness will be her undoing.

THIRTEEN

THE IMAGE IN the mirror seems distorted. He moves his face closer. The hideous totem of his nonsensical pursuit pulses like a beacon; his lip is bulbous and shiny with saliva and still throbbing. He dabs the area tentatively, mistrustful, with a swab of TCP. Squeezes his eyes at the sting, takes a quick breath and swears.

Maria will ask questions. Trudy will sulk. The class may snigger. All this is bad enough. And yet it is what *she* will think when she sees his disfigured mouth that darkens his mind every few seconds. Will she find him repulsive? He had left her at the pool, swimming and treading water, quietly floating on her back to watch him as he used his sleeve to staunch the blood. She seemed as passive as the pool itself; encapsulated in its dark, remote womb. He had not said goodbye; had simply hurried away, holding his cuff to his mouth, stopping now and again along the path to spit out blood.

He growls and shakes his head, and then in a sudden surge of rage takes the bottle of TCP and smashes it against the tiled floor of his bathroom. It is thanks to her that he now looks like a gargoyle. Thanks to her that he is losing his mind. Thanks to her, thanks to her!

But still he wants her.

'Jake?'

Maria. Like a hole in the head.

'What?'

'What was that?' He can hear her heavy tread – clip, thunk, clip, thunk; even a horse sounds more elegant – across the tiles towards the bathroom. Before he can wipe away the antiseptic she is standing in the doorway. In her platform shoes she looks like something out of *Equus*.

'Jesus Christ, what happened to your lip?'

'I cut it.'

'I can see that. How?'

'On the TCP bottle.'

'What?'

His mind races. But he is practised at this art. He can think on his feet. He can live by his wits. He must just keep talking.

'TCP bottle was jammed.' He looks doleful. 'I tried to open it with my teeth.' She continues staring. 'Stupid, I know. You've told me so many times not to do that.' *She's not buying it.* 'Anyway, next thing I knew I had broken it open and, well, it cut me and I dropped it on the floor.'

'Hmmm,' she says. 'Well, let's clear it up.'

She is reserving judgement, he thinks. She will make up her mind later. For now, she is being practical. This is what she does.

They cook dinner in silence, moving about the kitchen like shadow dancers. This nightly ritual – cut, chop, pop open the wine – is one he once savoured. It is these simple structures that provide frameworks. Support. Rhythm. Lay the table, soften the lights, light the candles, play some music.

'It's the little occasions that make life meaningful,' Maria used to say. 'Imagine if we died tomorrow and we hadn't used the good linen the night before?'

The notion had probably come from one of her self-help books, and yet it was something he once loved about her, this sense of celebration. Tonight he wishes he could draw some comfort from its flow.

She splashes Chardonnay into two large wine glasses. It gleams golden in the candlelight.

'Mmmm. Buttery. Delicious.' She hands him a glass. He takes a whiff and a sip and grimaces as the acid bites into his lip. She watches him very closely, refusing to acknowledge his pain.

'About the exhibition,' she says.

'What exhibition?'

'The one I plan on having in a few weeks' time. Do you have anything for me?'

'No.'

'What about the canvas you started a few months back? It's just sitting there. Why don't you give it a try again, Jake?'

'It's unresolved.'

'And I meant what I said about your students' work. I think we need to give them a taste of what it's like to go on show. Is there anything you can get to me by next week?'

'That's a ridiculous deadline, Maria.'

'I know. Just send me a few pieces. I've invited Frank. It's a good opportunity for your students to get some exposure.'

'I hate Frank.'

'You're supposed to. All artists hate critics. I know he can be cruel at times. But we have to have someone there from the *Cape Times*.'

Later in bed, as she closes her book and stretches to turn out the light, she turns to him.

'Jake?'

'Mmm.'

'What did you need the TCP for in the first place? Why were you trying to open that bottle?'

But his eyes are firmly closed. He could just as easily be asleep.

She returns to classes without apology, a silent spectre, unseeing, all-seeing. Whether painting, drawing or staring out of the window, she carries her void with her – its aura of forgetting, its vacant density repelling students like sulphur.

But Jake is not repelled. And nor, it seems, is the boy who stops to pick her up every afternoon. He has noticed the youngster once or twice before, waiting outside the school – only because he is rather conservatively dressed – but when he sees him open the passenger door of a white Mazda hatchback and watches Zara fold her long limbs into it, the young man takes on a new dimension of interest. Quite simply, and with almost immediate effect, he hates him.

Were the boy to have the first inclination that he has become the subject of this man's aversion, and were he then to understand why, a similar emotion would no doubt be generously returned, with increased, maybe doubled, intensity.

For he has lived in the shadows of this love since he first found her and watched her flapping her arms and singing 'Au Clair de la Lune' among the moss and the mud and the broken branches of their secret hideout. This is his world. His excavation. He was here first. First to love her, and ever since too. Surely that counts on the scales of justice? Surely history affords one a 'right'?

If he could pass through that membrane of light that separates this reality from the next, perhaps he might hear Camille speaking from that place of knowing, where the only death is of Time. Camille, who had been the only real mother figure he ever knew. So brief, so deep her mark on his young life before she died, that he often found himself talking to her, the way one might silently pray to God or Mother Mary.

In her voice like a river, now light with insight, he can almost hear her telling him not to hang his hopes too heavily on the twigs of justice or history, for politics is often just 'power tricks' said quickly. *Life is not always fair*, petit. And it is the same for love as it is for the land: often, it is the one with the silver tongue who gets the vote. Whether it is the hard teeth of destruction razing your home to the ground or a line of love whispered softly down your back, the landlords and the lovelords peddle the same power. One might dispossess you of your land, another of your heart. But whether it is the possession of a nation or a single soul, the hunger is the same, and those who feed on power will dispossess and reassess until the jackal is fed. Isn't that silly, *petit*? she might laugh. Don't they know that the jackal is always hungry? Because neither land nor the love of anyone but ourselves can truly be owned. And the only true 'rights' are never over anything but our own choices. *All you have to worry about, is whether* you *are fair*. The jackal may gorge himself on power until he is sick, but the contents of his stomach, however damaged by appetite and acid, will forever return to the earth undigested.

And still he can hear her voice speaking. You must understand, *petit*. Neither those who have loved the longest nor the deepest, nor those whose ancestors have rooted the land with the vegetation of their dreams and dug into the soil the turned leaves of their memories, are any closer by their wanting to having rights, or to getting what they justly deserve, than the lions and elephants that prowl and lurk in the hungry sun of wild country. Or the swollen-bellied orphans that crouch in the shadow of the vulture's wing, their saucer eyes emptied by starvation.

It is not easy for you, I know, she may continue. To pass through this thin skin that separates this reality from infinity. (Although what is it but your own thorns that says you can't?) But don't worry. And she would press the furrowed indent between his brows. All you have to do is stop. Stop long enough to breathe in the hum and raw rhythms of all that moves wild and free; wild arums and acacia trees, purple thunderstorms and the churn of the ocean, the fragrant mimosa and forests of proud pines, sloe-eyed genets and the salt-edged rasp of the gulls.

For in all that is wild and free, *petit*, you will hear not only my voice, but all who have gone before you, a chorus of nature with one tongue singing: that we are but guests of this earth, and in the end all things are moved along by the rivers and the wind.

FOURTEEN

THEY TRAVEL THE last stretch between Cape Town and the valley in silence. Camille stares at the road and the undulating landscape on either side, unseeing. Her father sucks on his pipe. As the Citroën curls slowly round the last bend and bumps along the grass and mud towards the cottage, she catches sight of Pieter's red bicycle propped up against the peeling wall, glinting and winking in the last spokes of daylight. Oh dear. If his mother finds out, he'll be in for another whipping. With a sigh she slides a glance towards the swing from where Blom's squeals are dipping in and out of their open windows. They are playing in the oak tree, all three, its gnarled branches suddenly made young by their smooth and nimble limbs.

She calls a greeting to them as she treads across the stones and weeds to the sturdy wooden door. Once inside, she lights the stove and pulls the kettle onto its lilac flame. Then lifts her bag from her shoulder, and takes it to her room. She stops in the doorway. The suitcase she reinstated at the top of the wardrobe that morning is now on the floor, fallen open to one side. Papers are strewn about like fine tissue paper. Light. Flimsy. The substance of a dream, without the paperweight of memory to curb its flight. An elaborate telltale trail of pink koki pen decorates the folder that had protected them. The string that held it all together has been snipped. *My love, how hard it is for me to write this letter* . . . The perpetrator slips like a shadow into the house behind her and folds warm and dirty arms around her mother's legs.

Zara now understands that a secret is something that is kept in a pumpkin-coloured folder in an old brown suitcase on top of the wardrobe. A secret is something that makes Maman angry and makes her eyes look like they do when she chops onions; full of big raindrop tears. A secret is a strange thing, because her maman is never angry with her. Not her maman. She gets angry with other people now and then, and sometimes even tells them what for. But never with her. She decides a secret cannot be a very good thing.

Two weeks later, when the baby recovers from meningitis and returns with its mother from hospital, the news starts to spread. Women in faded print dresses with scarf-clad heads are hanging out their washing on their makeshift washlines and telling each other about it. Gummy farm labourers, holding their caps on their pounding heads while stretching out their bony backs vertebra by vertebra, are discussing it. And on Sunday at church, the lady who leads the singing says a special thank-you to God that He should have seen fit to send them someone who can help heal their children, even if she does have a funny accent and it's hard to understand what she says.

But they are not the only ones. The Smits and the du Plessis – who have heard it from their servants – think it's irresponsible.

'I don't know what possessed you, Hermann,' says

his wife at the dinner table. 'To sell that property to those, those . . . strange people. I cannot stand it when foreigners interfere.'

Hermann nods his head and rolls his eyes in their veined sockets. 'The cottage was just sitting there, rotting, year after year. At least they've done something with it.'

'I always thought it was an outhouse,' giggles Martha du Plessis.

'It practically is,' says Ann Smit.

'Not a very hygienic place for a clinic then.'

'No, quite.'

'I see they painted the roof,' offers Hermann Smit. 'I'm telling you it looks a helluva lot better than it used to.'

'Oh, stop defending them like some bleeding heart liberal that you aren't,' snaps his wife.

'I heard Pieter was over there quite a bit.' Martha du Plessis is never averse to the odd provocation.

'Did you? That's ridiculous.' Ann Smit tightens her lips into a thin smile. 'Why ever would a crowd of gypsies interest a bright boy like him? He's off to boarding school next year, anyway. Bishops. It's too lonely for him here. May I pass you some more fillet?'

The Oliviers from the farm stall and curio shop told the de Goedes up the road that they think it's a good idea. They cannot understand why Camille would go to so much trouble. But they believe she has the love of the Lord in her heart, it's obvious, and that is an example to us all. They were even thinking of inviting her over for a *potjie*, until they heard she could not speak Afrikaans – which must explain why she doesn't come to church – and so didn't really see the point after all. But they smile at her all the same, which is easy to do with someone so pretty. Except for Sarel de Goede who takes his wife's arm whenever he sees Camille, and quickly looks the other way.

Camille has already spoken to a Dr Belotti from Groote Schuur Hospital, and been to visit his department to explain her requirements. Meeting him was the luck of the draw, or the hand of the gods, she cannot decide which. Convinced that she would be one in a long line of people wanting donations and help from this old city hospital, she decided not to bother with writing a letter, and took it upon herself to visit them in person. Who 'them' was she did not initially know. She would start with the registrar. He would know whom she should then speak to. On the day she drove into Cape Town, the registrar was at a conference in Bremen. His second in command was Dr Belotti. 'Luca Belotti,' his plump, pretty receptionist said carefully. 'He shouldn't be long. Take a seat.'

She sat for some time in a crowded waiting room, paging through old magazines. An Italian *Vogue*. In it, photos of elderly men, stylishly attired, holding the hands of taller, blonder teenagers, lips pouting.

She heard him before he reached the room. A man's voice singing all the way down the ward. '*Bel-la fanci-ulla . . . da da da dee-dah.*' And then a slim, dark-haired man in a white coat swept in, waving his hands as he walked through to his consulting room.

'*Pronto! Pronto!* Welcome! Is everybody happy? Who is first?' He had almost reached his consulting room when suddenly he took three steps backwards and turned to face her. '*Bella! Bella!*' he said, staring directly at her, shaking his head, before taking her hand, looking at it, kissing it, then marching back towards his rooms.

'That's Dr Belotti,' the dimpled nurse confirmed proudly over her shoulder as she followed him.

And suddenly, everyone was smiling.

When her turn came to speak to him, she found him helpful. And surprisingly professional. Only his hands, rather beautiful she thought, gave him away. They seemed to work together with his eyes, a powerful team, showing grave concern one moment, and undiluted flirtation the next. He nodded and smiled and agreed with her as she explained the difficulties of the local people in the valley. He wanted to help. He asked whether she would come back in a few days. He would see what he could do. Perhaps they could have lunch.

When she returned the following week, he was glowing with enthusiasm. He had twisted the arms of a few pharmaceutical reps, and organised a steady supply of free generic drugs. Just the basics: contraceptives, painkillers, antiseptics and some antibiotics. 'No antidepressants,' he said with a grin. 'This isn't the southern suburbs. Now how about something to eat?'

Within weeks the valley is full of static consternation. A newer, darker issue is brewing. Black people, uprooted from their hereditary land hundreds of miles away, are moving into the surrounding area, setting up makeshift shacks, shanties. Using anything they can get their hands on; from broken glass, black plastic bags, car tyres, bicycle wheels, bricks, stones, branches and mud, the squatting quarters are constructed. All around there are plastic bags stuck to bushes and barbed wire. Rubble living. An accident of civilisation. And disease. The men are being employed in the fruit factories, some even on the farms. And the women are asking the white madams for domestic jobs. 'I can't believe nobody is *doing* anything about it,' says Ann Smit. 'It's iniquitous. Next thing they'll be running the bloody country!'

But the ones who really despise the idea are the Coloureds.

'Was daai kaffir doing here?' Leah wants to know, after a young black woman, a baby wrapped snugly on her back, has knocked on the Smits' door looking for a job.

Ann Smit gives a little laugh. 'You Coloureds are such racists. It's so funny.'

Leah gives a knowing nod and hurls out the dirty water from the bucket.

'You mark my words. They're looking for trouble mos. Bringing their sickness en chilren en wanting our jobs. Haai.'

Doing something about it means building a wall around it, to stop the eyesore, until further steps can be taken. Overnight, the wall is awash with colour; graffiti art. And sprayed in black the words *Work for All*.

There is news of violence. A clash over the weekend. A black man knifed the first time. A Coloured man the second. Both dead.

'They're a bunch of drunken savages, the lot of them,' says Ann Smit. 'With a bit of luck the bad elements from both sides will kill each other off.'

Nobody knows how they heard, the people now living in shacks. But quite soon they too are visiting Camille. A steady trickle of indigents, the sick ones shuffling, oozing, sweating, bringing their ailments to her with the trust of children.

Most of it she finds she can treat on her own. Even the stitching up she does herself. But at least once a week there is a trip into Cape Town, to the hospital. At first they go in the Citroën. But thankfully, after a while, Dr Belotti persuades the members of the board at Groote Schuur to send a driver in one of the hospital Hi-Aces. And as this means the patients are no longer accompanied by Camille, Dr Belotti often comes to pick them up himself. When the Hi-Ace is unavailable he packs them into his sleek silver 1972 Mercedes sports car and drives them away. She knows people are probably watching this. She can almost sense their amazement. She cannot help but smile at the confusion this seemingly odd spectacle must cause in her neighbours' minds.

FIFTEEN

THE EXHIBITION DATE is fixed. So, it seems, is Maria's determination to involve his students. He mentions it to them cautiously, at the end of a lecture. From the immediate murmuring that this provokes, sticking their heads together with the hum of bees, he realises that this idea is welcome motivation. A chance for them to gauge their talent. To stretch their abilities. To gather together the pollen of inspiration and make honey. He glances at Zara. No heads tilt forward to conspire with hers. She simply sits staring straight back at him. But as he looks away, he thinks he sees her smile. Is it at him? Or the exhibition idea? He looks back. She looks down. But the vaguest memory of the smile, soft at the corners, still lingers.

'We'll begin working on the exhibition pieces tomorrow then,' he says, looking away. 'Please come with ideas.' And snapping his note file closed, he marches out of the room.

A while later he is checking e-mails in his office: invitations to book launches, to lunch at a wine estate, adverts for some online art publications, a note from Trudy downstairs at reception: *Miss you. When?*

The door handle turns. He looks up sharply; his small, round reading spectacles drop onto the bridge of his nose.

'Yes?'

But Zara is already inside. Serene as ever.

'I came to say goodbye.'

'Why? Where are you going?' He jumps to his feet. His car keys fall to the floor.

'Home.'

'Oh, yes. Home. Of course. Sorry, I thought for a minute you meant . . . thank you. Thank you for letting me know.' For a mad moment it occurred to him that she might mean she was leaving the school. It hit him in the guts. But no, of course that's not it. Why would she? His breath is becoming shorter. Another panic attack. *No, please! Surely not now?*

Yes, now.

It gets worse; his breath clenches, his lungs a fist of iron in his ribcage.

Death, dying, he is surely going to die! To suffocate.

'Please don't leave just yet,' he says. Even he can hear that his voice is higher than usual.

'Why?'

'Just stay. Please. A few minutes. I don't feel well. I have these . . . attacks. It would help me enormously if you just . . . stayed.'

She walks over to the window and looks out.

'Okay. Just a few minutes. Till my lift gets here.' Then she climbs into her chair, folds her legs under her and closes her eyes. He sits down, his hand on his heart. Blood gone mad. Racing. Erratic. Death or insanity squeezing his ribcage. *Breathe!* He reaches into his wallet for the small pack of white pills, the size of milk teeth, breaks one free and throws it into his mouth. Why doesn't she help him? Then, with his head in his hands, he breathes as slowly and as deeply as he can for several minutes.

As the panic eases he looks up. Why didn't she help him? Didn't she know how he needed her? Couldn't she see? He stares at her. She is asleep. Sound asleep! He is amazed. But also envious. The gift of living so exquisitely in the moment. The freedom of surrender into it. She looks so peaceful, eternal. Is that what sleep is: what we do each night for a lifetime to prepare us for death? In both, a residue of purity returns to the face. As though the soul in leaving the body – for a night or forever – takes with it the clots of memory and in exchange returns our infant hearts.

He stands up as quietly as he can. Through the window he can see the white Mazda grinding to a halt. He turns and watches her for a while longer.

'Zara,' he says gently, after some time. He does not want to repeat what happened the last time he woke her. She opens her eyes, yawns, then uncurls her legs and moves to the window, acknowledging the white Mazda with a silent nod to herself.

'I'm okay now,' he says.

'I know.' Then she bends to where he sits again on his chair, brushes her warm mouth against his cheek, and leaves.

All week the students work on their submissions. Work late into the evening, leaving a trail of cigarette butts and polystyrene cups, the dregs of turbid coffee still separating at the bottom. There is the low sound of music; they bring CDs, he brings an old player, a buzz of contented activity. And each day, all day long, he waits and watches for Zara to arrive. A hundred times he replays the last afternoon he saw her in his office: *I came to say goodbye.* She came especially to say goodbye. Does that mean something? Was it forever? Perhaps she didn't want to contribute anything to the exhibition. Then why didn't she say anything? *That is not her way.* Well, why not? Why the hell not?

He paces the floor between the easels. The clean smell of paint. Brushes bobbing. Stains everywhere. Where is she? Is she coming back? Every now and then, a student will put down a brush, stand back, reflect and ponder. Sometimes looking across to him, beckoning. 'Dr Coleman, would you mind giving me your opinion?'

By Wednesday he cannot bear it any longer. Tomorrow then. If she is not here tomorrow, he will go and find her. This resolution cheers him up a little. Having a plan. People need to have plans, or what is living for? Of course, it suddenly strikes him, he need not wait till tomorrow. Why should he, in fact? The idea gathers momentum, and at lunchtime he leaves the students painting, with the promise of returning later.

This time the drive there is easier. Even the bumps and potholes seem less obtrusive. He parks his car a little way from the Citroën. He has already decided not to bother the old man; he feels sure he will find her up the pathway, somewhere there. If truth be told, the wiry old bugger makes him feel downright uncomfortable. Something in the way his wraithlike body turned to face him the last time he was here. Something about the intense blue of his eyes, folded into his leathery, whiskery face. It makes him feel unusually young and silly.

He climbs the pathway, his good Italian shoes kicking up little puffs of dust. As he reaches the top of the bank, he sees her in the distance, sprawled on the grass under a tree. There is another young woman too, a Coloured girl. He waits for her to see him. The dog barks, and they swing their heads in his direction, but do not beckon or wave. He hesitates. Then he makes his way over nonetheless.

'Hello,' he says.

'Hello,' says the Coloured girl. 'Who are you?'

'Jake,' he says, sitting down on the grass. 'And who are you?'

'Blom. I'm Blom September. What are you doing here?'

He smiles at her forthright manner. She is rather pretty.

'I've come to shout at your friend. She's been bunking class.'

Zara has neither moved nor acknowledged his presence.

'Well, then you can jus' bugger off to where you came from,' says Blom. But before he can take offence she gives a squeal of delight, her small teeth white and straight against her brown skin.

'Jus' pulling your leg, man. I have to go anyways. I've just come back here after being away, so I wanted to see my friend. My sister.' She grins at Zara. 'But I promised my ma I'd help her with some washing. She's like the devil's own soul sister that one, always giving me work.' She rises to her small bare feet. 'So bye.'

'Bye.' He cannot help smiling. Watches her skip along the path, her short red skirt bouncing as she walks. Halfway along she stops, turns round and shouts, 'Zara, see you later. Your house. With Pieter.' Then gives a little wave before disappearing down the bank. He turns to Zara, still spreadeagled on the grass, her head lazily resting on her arms, the dog resting his head on her buttocks.

Pieter?

'What's this about?' he says. 'Why are you not at class?'

'What for?'

'Well, the rest of them are preparing for the exhibition. Don't you want to be a part of that?'

'Yes.'

'Well then? I don't understand.'

'I have something to submit already. I prefer to work on my own. It's better that way.'

'I wish you'd told me.' He tries to sound firm.

She remains silent.

He changes tack. 'I was worried.'

He stretches himself out alongside her on the grass, lying on his side, his hand propping up his head. Through the leaves he watches clouds coagulate into little clusters. An eggbox sky.

'Would you like to swim?'

'Not after last time, quite frankly, no.'

'Still scared of blood then?' He detects a spot of sympathy in her tone. Or is she mocking him?

'Maybe we should avoid that topic this time. It's a beautiful day.'

She stares directly at him for some time. Motionless.

'Zara, what happened to your mother?'

'She died.'

'Was she ill?'

'I don't remember.'

'Were you very young?'

'I don't know. I suppose so.'

He adjusts his head on his hand. She looks up.

'Death is the mother of Beauty. I read that some-where,' she says.

'Do you agree?'

She does not answer.

'Give me your hand,' she says after a while, rolling

143

over with the easy suppleness of a cat. She lifts her T-shirt, unfolds his fingers, then moves them slowly over her belly.

'Blood temperature,' she whispers. 'Life.'

Her warm skin against his hand. Is this an invitation? An initiation? Or simply her idea of conversation? He tries not to shake. 'Life,' he repeats, anxious not to lose the connection. *Does he dare?* With the flat of his hand barely touching her skin, he can just perceive the soft indentations pressed into her from the grass. Then her hand falls away and he continues the crossing unguided. Slowly. Softly. Half expecting her to attack him. Stopping now and then to make sure. Each second of his tentative exploration as fragile as the last. Each tiny tremor of response a victory. The subtlety with which her body dips and rises and curves and folds and flows. To be won over and worshipped first with his fingertips, with the awe of a child. *May I touch?* Then with his mouth, his teeth, his cheek, his tongue. And later – when their bodies have become less separate, more fluid – with the firmness of a man. Deeper and deeper into her light he enters. Into her otherness; the world across the great divide.

She abandons herself to pleasure with the same ease as she gives herself over to sleep, he reflects as he drives home. And yet there is something troubling him. Something incomplete. Something in her eyes. Or something not in her eyes, something missing. Yes, it is this: in spite of her blood-warm body, her eyes, even in lovemaking, remain devoid of emotion. It is this about the afternoon that disturbs him. Unnerves him. Even unmans him. When he unmasks his shallow victory, he is left knowing that only when he can possess this, the hollow in her eyes, ignite that soul's life spark, that the true surrender, with all her sweet foreignness, will be his. All else is mockery.

The old man is cooking a big stew with a bag of vegetables he has bought from the Coloured vendors who sell them dirt cheap off the main road. The women get them each day from the big market in the next village, leaving early in the morning in an old bakkie to stock up. The produce is often misshapen and still caked with earth. This pleases him; he completely mistrusts the more perfect supermarket options packed in polystyrene and cellophane. There is something too contrived about their obvious symmetry, compelling him to declare them flavourless on principle. Back in France buying fresh vegetables every other day was a way of life. Digging them out of big baskets, examining them, knowing which shape and colour would have the most flavour. These are the things he misses. The things he would love to take Zara back to one day. As soon as number thirteen comes in again . . . He hands Zara some carrots and a knife, then throws the crumbs from the breadboard out of the window before handing it to her.

'We cook for Blom and Pieter also?' he asks, waiting for her nod.

Blom who has been away for four years. To the Karoo, to an aunt, where she looked after the children. She had left quite suddenly, leaving an unfamiliar silence in her wake. Like a little bird that has taken its incessant chatter elsewhere for the summer and decided, against the laws of nature, not to return. Blom with her springy childhood hair and fingernails like little monkey nuts, now suddenly back, no longer fourteen but eighteen. The sharp edges of adolescence rounded. Her humour intact.

And Pieter. The man-child with the square face and chin stubble, who has never left. Not even when he was sent away to boarding school as a child. Not even when he was forbidden to come over to play and beaten savagely. Somehow, like a stray dog, he always manages to find his way back to the cottage with the peeling plaster walls. To Zara.

There they are now, bumping into each other again for the first time in four years. He can see them from the window. Blom gives him a kiss. He scratches his head and nods, unsure what to do. His short hair still sticks up at the crown even though he now shaves every day. And his shoulders have grown broader, from the sport, from rugby. If she were to look closely, she might see a few strands of chest hair curl around the neck of his T-shirt. They come walking towards the cottage, Pieter carrying his discomfort in long loping strides, the pretty young brown woman bobbing at his side oblivious. The old man smiles to himself, then yawns. He thinks he'll turn in early tonight. As soon as the youngsters leave. He has been feeling a little tired of late.

difference. In Italy, there are many doctors. Here, you know your contribution counts. Here, you have the opportunity to save many lives. To be God. Oh, I like that! And after I comb the beach, when I get into bed every night – well, sometimes not *every* night – I say to myself, I say: Luca, you are a beautiful man.' He roars with laughter. 'And then I sleep, full of my own goodness.' He gives a full, mock sigh and smiles at her. 'Doesn't that make you sick?'

'What beach do you comb?'

'The one in front of my little house. It's incredible what you find.'

'You live on the beach?'

'Yes. And each evening I rake the sand. I have found the most beautiful pieces of wreckage, ceramics, even a woman's glass button, all from shipwrecks. Everything washes up on the shore in the end. Would you like to come and see it?'

Leah now takes a short cut past the back of the cottage on her way to work. Camille goes out to meet her the following day.

'It's called the Wynboerevereniging,' Leah explains in reply to her question. 'They all sit round a moerse big table and discuss their staff like we're a troop of baboons. I know. When it's Meneer Smit's turn to host, I have to go along and serve bobotie and stuff for the *poephols*. They won't listen to you. I know. They just won't.'

'They might. If they think they are getting something out of it.'

'And what exactly they get out of it?'

'Healthy workers. Higher productivity.'

'Pfffff. Ja. Okay, you give it a try. But don't be

disappointed. They're befok in die kop. Fucked in the head. And another thing . . .'

'Yes?'

'Pieter. Blom says he's coming to your house again.' She presses her hands together. Tensed. Thick veins branch up into her wrists.

'Yes, he was here the other day. I was in Cape Town. I didn't know.'

'Well, that mother of his will make sure that fat pig sjamboks the Jesus out of him if she knows. I heard her telling him he mustn't go near Hotnots. When he asks why, she says we'll give him some disease. I think it's better he doesn't come over.'

'What a charming woman.' She sighs. 'Leah? Your eye. Is it okay?'

'What do you mean?'

'It looks bruised. Did he hit you again?'

'If I want help I'll ask for it. I got a tongue in my head, haven't I?'

When she returns to the house she finds Zara still in her pyjamas pressed up against the front wall, a Coloured man in torn overalls cornering her, sneering at her, only a few feet away. Laika is snapping at his heels, making him jump. He pretends it is part of a dance, then gives Laika a good kick, sending him whimpering to Zara.

'What on earth are you doing?' says Camille.

'Haai, lady.' The man lifts his cap, then drops it with a little plop on to his head. He runs bloodshot eyes appreciatively over her body, grinning at her with his gums. 'Jy't a figure like a trigger.'

'Get out. Now!'

'But I'm sick. Isn't this where to come if I'm sick?' The drunken man grins at her, deliberately acting simple. In three strides she marches directly up to him and pushes him as hard as she can. He reels and starts retching, looking up to see an old man coming from the house with a stick. *'Jislaaik!'*

'Get out!' Camille orders, picking up a nearby rock. 'Before I damage you.'

They watch him sway and turn and zigzag his way out. At the gate he lifts his cap and drops it on to his head again. Then, holding it on his head with one hand, he turns and gives an elaborate bow, loses his balance and falls, before disappearing from their view. Zara is still stiff against the wall.

'What happened, Zara? Tell Maman.'

'Wait. Laika. He kicked Laika.' She drops down to wrap herself around the dog.

'Laika's okay. I promise. Now come, Zara, you must tell me what happened.'

'He said he wanted to see my broekies. Broekies, like what Blom calls them. My panties. I said no. I said these are my pyjamas and I don't wear broekies with my pyjamas. And then he started to come closer. I don't know why.'

Drunk at seven o'clock in the morning. That may be his business. But inflicting it on Zara is quite another. The shock is such that at first Camille has no way of knowing how to contain herself. Nor how to keep her anger and her fear from Zara.

When she mentions it to Leah, she simply shrugs. 'It could have been worse,' is all she has to say.

'Exactly!' says Camille. 'So what am I supposed to do? Wait until something does happen before I do anything about it?'

'It's life. You'll get over it.'

'It is *not* life. Not life as I know it anyway.'

'Well, if you want to stay here you better get used to it. What makes you think you so special? Here, everybody pays sometime or another.'

She spends the day pacing, muttering to herself. She has to force herself to be gentle with her patients, and is still fuming at dinner time.

'Let it go, Camille,' says her father when Zara goes to take a bath. 'It's going to make you sick if you don't. I don't think he'll be back. He's just a drunken fool.'

'Will you watch Zara for me?' she responds. 'I need to go for a walk. I think I may go for a swim at the dam. Maybe that will help.'

The Wynboerevereniging is scheduled to meet that Thursday evening. Leah knows that Meneer Smit keeps his appointments in a big diary, in the study. The host: Meneer Anton du Plessis. The time: 7 p.m. She will walk with Camille to show her where Anton du Plessis's farm is. They plan to get there a little early so that Camille can speak to Meneer du Plessis first.

'Most probably they'll meet in the tasting room,' she says. 'Bit of luck they'll get a bit sozzled and then you can tell them anything you like and they'll agree.'

Meneer du Plessis is not a small man. He has a sleek look of wealth rather like a well-groomed, well-fed domestic animal. 'Carries his money in his stomach,' Leah said before leaving her there. But in spite of his size, Camille finds him disarmingly gentle.

'How can I help you, madam?'

She explains about the clinic. 'I would like an opportunity to tell you about what I am doing, and why. It would be wonderful if I could have the support of the community.'

'The agenda has already been typed up,' he says. 'But

seeing as you have come all this way, and on foot, I'm sure we can give you a chance to speak. May I get you something to drink while you wait?'

There is still a pocket of time before the others arrive; she had not expected to find the farm so easily. She toys with her wine glass. A Coloured woman arrives with a big pot of bredie. Camille smiles at her. It is not returned. She thinks again of the man who taunted Zara and turns to Meneer du Plessis, who is filling a glass of wine for himself.

'Maybe you can help me; I'm unfamiliar with customs here. What exactly is this *dopstelsel*?'

'*Dopstelsel*? It's an old Afrikaans term for "tot system". It used to be a way of paying labourers, but it shot us in the foot in the end.'

'What do you mean?'

'Well, nobody seems to know what came first, the tot system or the dependency. All we know is that our Coloured workforce are mad about wine. They'll do anything for it. Some would actually *prefer* to be paid in wine, if you can believe that. And if you don't give it to them, they'll pinch it, or buy it in jerrycans from the shebeens down the road. So in some ways, we prefer to give it to them; at least we know they're not drinking *witblits* or paraffin. And they only get it after a day's work, so it keeps them sober during the day.'

'I suppose it's naive to think there could be some kind of rehabilitation programmes introduced.'

Meneer du Plessis smiles at this thought. A broad, honest smile.

'This is wine country. Somehow I can't see *anybody* in this industry, whether they are black, brown, white or purple, standing up in front of their friends, neighbours and colleagues and saying, "My name is Anton du

Plessis and I'm an alcoholic."' He gives a deep laugh. Gently tries to explain it to her. 'You see, Miss Camille, here wine is a way of life. It's part of our identity. But I do understand your concern, naturally. We must worry about these things and keep an eye on it, of course.'

In clouds of dust they arrive. Some in big trucks with big tyres. Some in Mercedes-Benzes and BMWs. There is handshaking and laughter and wine poured from bottles without labels. She remains seated. At various points each of the men walks across to her and introduces himself. They are friendly and kind. Each of them asks whether she has had some wine. A few want to know whether she is comfortable on the hard tasting bench. One even fetches a pillow from his car. When Mr Smit arrives, he greets his neighbours quickly, before making a beeline for her.

'Hello, Mr Smit.' She smiles politely.

'What a lovely surprise!' he fawns, showing his bad teeth. 'Do you have some wine? Are you comfortable?'

At her simple nod, he returns to the circle of men and their conversations, casting sly glances in her direction when he thinks she's not looking.

At 7.30 p.m. Meneer du Plessis motions everybody to sit down and charge their glasses for the meeting. He introduces Camille and tells them that she will be speaking to them at the end of the meeting, apologises for not having it on the agenda.

'Can I not get it over with quickly and leave you men to your meeting?' she asks.

'No, madam, because somebody needs to take you home. You can't walk around at night here any more. Not with all these new blacks about.'

The meeting is interminably long. Most of it is in Afrikaans, which she does not understand. She listens to the sound of its guttural, earthy flow. It is a language with emotion, that seems to bend in tone to the nature of the man uttering it. In the mouth of a soft-spoken man with a low-timbre voice it resonates beyond the ear, words running smoothly into each other, like poetry. From the mouth of another farmer it sounds like a rough weapon. A blunt implement. Something from which you would want to escape. Even though she does not follow it, she cannot imagine these large-boned men, their powerful frames, their strong jaws speaking anything else. It would be hard to imagine them speaking in a tongue as delicate, as yin, as French. It is a masculine language, no doubt very precise. Handcrafted for the people by the people. With special phrases and words that you would need to be Afrikaans to appreciate fully. She watches them nod or disagree with gusto. Speakers of the code unite. It seems some new ideas are welcomed with slaps on the back, others with jolly laughter. A man takes notes. When it is at last her turn to talk she stands. Grips her hands in front of her and explains why she has set about opening a clinic, and that she needs funds to build another room on her property for this purpose. She has gathered some quotes for each suggested option.

'But we already have a clinic. It's very good, I'm told,' someone says.

'I'm sure it is very good. But it's not enough any more,' she says. She can feel her heart thumping. 'The needs of the local people far exceed the current commitment of the clinic. Most accidents, if you want to look at them that way, happen outside of clinic hours. We need something more immediate.'

'Always used to be enough,' the same man says. 'Trouble is they breed like flies. Don't see why it should be our problem.'

'There's also people going to the clinic who shouldn't be here,' says another. 'I don't think we should increase facilities at all. It will only encourage them.'

'Not only that,' says a third farmer. 'But I've heard rumours that those bloody natives in their shacks are coming to you too. The last thing I want is to give them any reason to stay. Pardon my language.'

Mr Smit doesn't say a word. Avoiding eye contact with anybody, he produces a chunk of biltong, shaped a bit like Africa, from a packet. Then takes a Swiss army knife from his jacket and slices it in clean, quick strokes, before passing it around.

'But as long as they *are* here, surely it is better for everybody if they are healthy,' she says.

'Is it? It's nature's way of keeping the population down. We shouldn't interfere.'

'I don't think we should just write it off,' says Meneer du Plessis. Mr Smit nods vigorous assent. 'You know, wine farming is not a quick career choice for any of us, Miss Camille. We've been here for generations. And so have our workers. They are born here. They die here. They are like our family, we try to look after them.'

'Ja, that's true. That's how it is,' nods Mr Smit.

'Then I don't understand,' she says.

'You're not from here. It can't be easy to learn our ways.' He smiles at her kindly.

'They're a bit like children,' explains another. 'They look to us like we're their parents. We care for their families, feed them, house them, bury them. It's not an easy job. But there's no getting away from the fact that sometimes they can act like savages. And they love wine. That's just how it is. If we don't give it to them they'll either steal it, or have to buy it. And then their families will never see the money. So what do you do?'

'Pay them more?' It falls out her mouth before she can stop herself. The men stare at her, amazed.

'They'll only buy more wine. We have to be responsible. We give them housing, educate them, medicate them. If we give them too much rope, they'll hang themselves. If you had been here as long as we have you would understand that.'

Camille sits down.

Meneer du Plessis looks concerned. 'Listen, gentlemen, the lady has come across specially to tell us all about it. Least we can do is think about it.'

'No, sure, of course,' says Mr Smit.

'We'll put it on the agenda to talk about next month. Okay?' Meneer du Plessis smiles at her. 'You leave the figures with us.' He hands the paper with the carefully tabulated numbers to the man who is taking notes. 'Now, tonight's meeting is adjourned. Who can give the lady a lift home?'

'It's fine. Really. I'll walk. It's not far. I enjoy it.'

'I'll take her,' says Mr Smit. 'I live nearby.' He puts his hand on her back as she walks out into the dark, the way a gentleman would guide a lady out of a room to his car. She can feel his palm hot and sweaty through her shirt. In the ambiguous dark he slides his fat fingers under her armpits and digs them ever-so-slightly into her breast. It could have been accident, she later thinks. He could simply be clumsy. But at the time she does not wait to think. She spins around like a whip, the *thwack* of her hand cutting through the night. Two of the men framed by the doorway of the tasting room stop and stare. Watch as she slips, like a doubt, into the dark shadows. Hear him swear, slam his car door and drive off at speed.

SEVENTEEN

THERE IS ONLY a week left before the exhibition. Some of the students are fretting and fussing. Others are relaxing deeper and deeper into their inspiration, mining the depths of their ability with passion and joy. He himself alternates between feeling confused and frustrated. The memory of his afternoon with Zara creeps into every thought. Normally, a conquest such as this would leave him feeling buoyant. Elated even. Not more frustrated than before, with a hundred gnawing doubts clawing at his mind. And worst of all, completely at a loss as to what to do next. There is the obvious drive, the need to repeat the afternoon in the hope that at some point he will truly engage her. But there is also a nagging suspicion that she is mocking him. Exactly how he can't be sure. He can't figure it out. The only good news – and he hopes it *is* good news – is that he too has started a painting. A new one. He thinks he may even like it. With a bit of luck it will be ready for the exhibition. A drawcard for the public.

Maria will have to liaise with Trudy directly in the week to come, to arrange transportation of the paintings to the gallery. That should be interesting. Two jealous women. He rather likes the idea. Although it could be dangerous. He doesn't think he'll get involved. He has enough on his plate, and tells her as much.

'I trust you are arranging transport for the paintings.'

'Yes, of course. But I am going to need some information beforehand. For the pamphlets and the press.'

'Speak to Trudy.'

'Can't wait.'

Maria knows that she is taking a big risk. Her reputation is at stake each time she holds an exhibition; although in this case, she is hoping that the political gain from hosting a student exhibition and promoting the undiscovered will outweigh the potential negative impact of any artistic immaturity. But the bigger risk goes beyond reputation. The bigger risk is that by taking her suspicions and holding them under the spotlight, she may glean far more than she is ready to know.

Is one ever ready, she wonders, to find out whether one's worst suspicions are true? Or that a dream has died, long, long before it was born? A dead foetus cannot remain in the womb for very long before it poisons the bearer. Nor a dead dream in the heart.

Unbeknown to Jake, she has already spoken to Trudy about the exhibition. In her professional capacity she has the confidence to handle matters like these with ease. Trudy was cool and clipped and equally professional. Very helpful, but distant. The real test will come at the exhibition itself. Trudy will have to attend, to facilitate and help organise. Then she will be able to see the two of them together. She doesn't know what she is looking for. But she knows that she will recognise it like an old enemy when she sees it.

Towards the end of the week Zara returns to class. She brings a painting with her, plus some wood and a small drawstring bag of tools. At the end of the lecture, when the group return to their own paintings, she sets about making a frame. He walks past her again and again. She gives him no acknowledgement whatsoever. It is as though he does not exist. She simply sets about measuring and cutting, pursing her lips to hold one or two sharp nails as she constructs the frame. And yet there is something different about her. For the first time since he has known her – such a short time, yet forever – she has brushed her hair, and tied it back, away from her face, with some coarse string. The absence of expression from her face now more accentuated than ever. After some time she removes her baggy shirt and works in what appears to be a man's vest. He finds himself staring at the skin on her shoulders, brown and smooth, the top of her back, her nipples brushing the front of the fabric. At the end of the day, when he can stand it no more, he says in a low voice, 'See me in my office, okay? I'd like to review your painting.'

She does not respond. He tells himself not to panic. This is how she is, that's all. He will go and sit quietly in his office and wait.

He leaves the door slightly ajar. In case she gets the wrong impression and thinks he's not there. Switches on his computer and absent-mindedly checks his e-mail. After a few minutes he checks his watch. Then the door. A green fly perched in a triangle of sunlight rubs its feet together in glee. He stands up and begins to pace. As he glances out the window, he sees the white Mazda hatchback driving away. She has left then. And God alone knows when she'll be back. He wants to scream. Picks up the 'stress ball' Maria bought him and throws it as hard as he can against the wall.

There is a small knock at the door. Trudy. For the

first time, Trudy too is becoming complicated. To date he could always rely on her to add lightness to any situation. To smooth the rough edges and warm the cold ones. And yet she seems to have changed lately. He doesn't know what's got into her. She keeps leaving cryptic messages on his voicemail. *'Call me. Remember me?'* And lurking around his office waiting to grab hold of him on his way in or out. And she's not looking good either. He finds it amazing how quickly women can lose their looks if they don't pay attention. He can't help feeling a little disappointed. Trudy has always been one of the best-groomed women he has ever met. But she appears to have lost weight; her flesh doesn't seem to fit her, or something. She has a haggard look. Most annoying of all, she keeps crying. He was going to ask her out for lunch yesterday, but when he saw the rings under her eyes and her silly attempt at blinking back tears he changed his mind. What he needs right now is positive reinforcement. Not a guilt trip.

'Yes, love,' he says. He wishes she would just leave him alone.

'Just wanted to tell you that some people called from Holland,' she says. She is unusually pale.

'What about?'

'They want to come and see you next Tuesday. They spoke about commissioning you, something about an exhibition. It wasn't a good line and I couldn't work out their accents too well.'

'Did you set up a time?'

'Yes. Nine o'clock.'

'Fine. Thank you.'

This could be something. Maria must tell the press. Send a photographer. Maybe with that kind of goal, the muse will return.

'I haven't seen you in a while,' she says. 'Is there something wrong?'

'You've seen me. I've been around. Don't be silly, you've seen me every day!'

'You know what I mean.'

'Trudy, you of all people should know how busy I've been.'

'That's never got in the way before.' She seems so small suddenly. Like a hurt animal. Her eyes blister with tears. Shit! He rises out of his chair and takes her by the shoulders.

'You look tired. You've been working too hard. And you're right. I'm sorry. I've just been so snowed under. But I'll make it up to you as soon as the exhibition is over. Okay?'

'Okay.' She tries to smile.

'Maybe we can go away some place and relax?'

'That would be nice.'

'I have to go now. I'll think of something and let you know.'

He takes his keys, kisses her and briefly holds her tight, her petite frame suddenly so frail and delicate against him.

'Tomorrow,' he says as she turns to leave. He will think about what to say tomorrow. Right now he needs a stiff drink.

He drives for some time. He wants a pub where nobody will recognise him. He does not want conversation. There are too many cars outside his usual haunt in Constantia. He keeps driving. It is drizzling by the time he reaches the old fishermen's town of Kalk Bay. Salt spray and drunks. He thinks of his painting of the Coloured woman he had seen here, now hanging on

Cecily's wall. Maybe he'll find inspiration here again.

Inside the bar he knocks back a double whiskey, orders another and stares glumly out of the window. The rain. *She smells like the rain.* No! This cannot continue. Zara has addled his brain. Worse than that, she is toying with him. He cannot allow it. Will not allow it. Not from any woman. And especially not from somebody no more than eighteen or nineteen. Besides, it is now spilling over to his other relationships, and hurting people. Imagine if people got to hear about it! He would be the laughing stock. It must stop. How silly he has been. Funny how everything people say about midlife rings true one time or another. Must be that. Must be his way of buying a sports car. He looks around. Takes another slug. The room is swelling with smoke and voices. But nobody bothers him. Through the glitter-sprayed window cellophane waves crumple in the fairy lights, and foam, foam and beer and regulars slurring, laughing, beering, leering in the glow, while wet wind whips at the windows and cars slice along the inky roads, slippery as fish. He does not belong. He pays for the drink and leaves. On his way home he phones Maria.

'Let's go out for a bite.'

'That'd be nice. Where?'

'Don't know. You choose. Something you'd really like.'

He is starting to feel better. The sea air has done him good. He may even do some painting later.

The following morning he is in his office collecting notes when she walks in.

'Yes, Zara.'

'You wanted to see me?'

'That was yesterday.' He can feel his new resolve slipping from him like water.

'Oh. Okay.' She moves to leave.

'Wait!' It's an automatic reflex. His eyes dart from her to the door and back to her. She stops.

'I do need to see you. Will you come at lunchtime?'

'Okay.'

'Will you bring your painting?'

'I don't have it here.'

She walks away. A few hours later she is back. He walks towards her as she walks in, reaching one arm out to push the door shut behind her. He moves closer to her. She does not move away or adjust the space between them. That is one of the little things he notices about lovemaking; it eradicates the magic circles surrounding people. As though there has been some universal adjustment of sacred space. He leans forward to kiss her. She does not respond.

'Zara,' he whispers. 'Don't you want to kiss me today?'

'No,' she replies.

He is taken aback. 'No? Why?'

'Not here.'

'Why?'

She shrugs.

He sighs. 'Then where? *When?*'

'I don't know.'

'Tomorrow? In your neck of the woods?'

'Okay.'

'*Beyond rightdoing and wrongdoing, there is a field. Meet me there.* One of my favourite quotes. Rumi.'

But she does not respond. 'Is that all?'

'*All?*' He is amazed. Belittled. 'Yes, I suppose so.'

As she turns to walk away he doesn't know whether he wants to sing or to cry.

EIGHTEEN

THERE IS LITTLE time to ponder. Each day brings with it new faces, new challenges, new illnesses. And worries. Three patients she has seen she suspects have TB. She worries about sending them back to their shacks clutching their little bottles of pills. Worries that if she tells them to return so that she can take them to hospital for tests they may not. She worries about the germs coming into the tiny cottage. Twice a day she scrubs the place with disinfectant. It makes her hands swollen and chapped. She encourages Zara to play outside. But since the incident with the drunk at seven in the morning, she feels uneasy about Zara going too far from her sight.

A large black woman with undulating hips and enormous sagging breasts limps in with a gash on her foot. It is too late for stitches; the wound has already knitted itself coarsely together, seeping and weeping, infected.

'The sangoma, he give me things to put on, but they not working.' She has a powerful voice. The kind one can already hear singing.

'Sangoma?'

'Witch doctor. He throw bones and spirits tell him what is wrong.'

'I see. Well, the spirits should have told him that you need an antiseptic. You should have had stitches, but it's too late for that now. Sit here while I clean the wound and inject you.'

The foot is cracked and filthy, with toughened toenails caked with clay, mud and blood. She scrubs it in a bowl of Dettol. Then injects antibiotic into the wound. The woman screams ferociously and rolls her eyes like a crazed animal. Camille bandages it up and asks her to come back in a few days.

The black woman does not return in a few days. Instead, two black men arrive at the cottage; the first tall and angular, with wide eyes and nose, and skin pulled tight over strong bones. The second shorter with narrow eyes and a prominent mouth. She is busy dispensing a packet of contraceptives to a young Coloured woman.

'Wait on the bench,' she calls. 'I won't be long.'

Perhaps they do not understand, or do not hear, but they continue to stand, looking through the windows now and again.

After some instructions and explanation to the young woman, who shifts from one leg to the other, pulling the skin on the back of her arm with her fingers, she is free to speak to them. She washes her hands and appears at the door, wiping them on a small towel.

'Yes?'

'Want work,' the shorter one says.

'What kind of work?' *Where is Zara?*

'Any work. Painting. Garden. Building.'

'Do you know how to build? I mean, if I wanted a room built, would you know how to do it?'

'I work for builder in Cape Town. He go oversea. I know building.'

'I might need some building done. I'm waiting to hear if I'm getting some money. Can you come back?'

He nods.

'In a couple of weeks, or so?'

'Yes, ma'am.' He dips his head then mumbles something in Xhosa to his mate, and starts to move away. The second man does not move.

'Thank you,' says Camille, an attempt at closing the interaction.

'Food. I hungry,' says the taller man.

'Wait. I'll make you sandwich,' she says, disappearing into the cottage.

Where is Zara? Laika?

She quickly assembles the peanut butter sandwich and grabs an apple.

When she turns round the tall man is in the house. She gives a cry and jumps. At this point she hears the welcome groan of the Citroën, the rasp of the handbreak. The tall man looks towards the source of the sound, before taking his sandwich and walking out. He leaves the apple behind.

At the sound of the car, Zara too reappears from behind the house followed by Laika, tail wagging and held high to greet the old man.

'You're covered in paint,' says Camille, trying to hide her relief. 'Papa, just look at her. She's covered in paint!'

Her heart is still beating too powerfully to note the edges of guilt spreading across the child's face.

'Who was that?' the old man enquires. 'Patients?'

'No. They were looking for work. Hungry.' She does not want to infect him with her fear.

'Ah. Zara, what are you painting?' he enquires.

'Nothing.'

'I see nothing has a lot of colours. Where are you painting this colourful nothing?'

She pulls at her plait with smudgy fingers.

'Maybe round the back of the house? Can I come and have a look at this nothing that needs so much paint?'

'No.'

'No? Why not?'

'I'm busy. It's not finished.'

'That's okay. Sometimes it's good to see "work-in-progress".' He tries to engage her eyes, but they will not meet his. He cannot swap a twinkle.

'Come, let's make some tea,' says Camille. Her relief at seeing Zara safe outweighs any small crime she may be in the process of committing. 'Zara, would you like some juice?'

'We'll be inside just now,' the old man says, taking Zara by the hand. 'But first, young lady, take me to your leader.'

The back of the house is a riot of colour. Indefinite shapes and squiggles and dots stretch from the one end to the other.

'Hmmm,' he says. 'Very nice.'

'Can you see the birds?' she asks.

'Birds? Let me see. Is this a bird?'

'It's flying.'

'Ah, yes. And this one too?'

'It's eating.'

'And the spots?'

'That's the food that Maman gives them. I want them to know that we give them food. That they mustn't be hungry.'

'I see. Like a billboard.'

'A what?'

'An advertisement. For birds.'

'No. It's a letter. A bird letter.'

'Ah, naturally. A much better way of looking at it. Now let's go inside and try to explain this to your mother.'

Two weeks later, the woman with the cut foot returns. Staggers in, propped between two friends who sigh and sweat under the weight of her. The foot is no longer bandaged, and from the door Camille can see it is septic.

'Why did you not come back like I told you?'

The woman rolls her eyes.

'How am I to help you if you won't listen to me?'

'Sangoma put spell on me if I come to this house.'

'What?'

'Sangoma say white people they know nothing. White woman is worse. Know nothing. Is bad. Sangoma take off bandage and give me this to put on.' She hands Camille a closed jar with some dark paste inside. As Camille opens the jar the smell of stinking animal blood fouls the air, catching convulsively in her throat and nose. She closes it immediately and tosses it into a large black garbage bag.

'Look. I don't know if I can save your foot. You're going to have to wait here and I'll see if I can get you into Cape Town to see a doctor later this afternoon. What the sangoma said to you was more than stupid. It might mean you have to have your foot cut off.'

'*Hawu*!' She says. 'Oh my God.' She rolls her eyes, the whites veined and creamy. The other two women shake their scarved heads like chorus members in a Greek tragedy, making clicking sounds of disapproval.

Dr Belotti works late into the night operating on the foot he tries to save. Camille watches him work. His hands slow and careful. But when he sees how deeply the rot has eaten away the flesh, he is left with no choice but to amputate, before the infection spreads any further.

'Just when you think it can't get more bizarre, it does,' she says the following afternoon to Dr Belotti, pushing the hair away from her face. 'It started out as a bad cut. If she'd listened – to me, not a witch doctor! – she'd have been all right.'

'You're tired, *bella*,' he says. 'Me too. I'm not working late today. Would you join me for a late-afternoon walk on the beach?'

Later, as she makes her way down to the shore she can see a man raking the sand. Round and round. A Zen garden on the beach. Then suddenly, he lifts the rake and dances the tango with it. From the wooden steps she can hear him sing.

'Hello!' she shouts.

He waves enthusiastically. Unashamed. 'Come down!'

The house is old and dilapidated and seems balanced precariously between two palms. Every room has a door which opens to the beach. The sun is dipping, retracting its warmth. A couple of die-hard, wet-suited surfers bob up and down in the waves. Luca has flung an old, bottle-green, fold-up mattress and a thick blanket on to the sand. A kitten rubs against her.

'I found him in the gutter,' says Luca. 'He loves the beach.'

A little later, to celebrate the rising moon, Luca brings rum cocktails and a plate of biscuits, bread, cheeses and smoked salmon. In the dark, the kitten rushes up and down a palm. Spiky. Electric. The sea extends long, foamy fingers up the pale beach, clawing at the sand, as though wishing to escape before Neptune drags it reluctantly back home.

'Do people in the northern hemisphere see the moon upside down?' Camille asks, leaning back and closing her eyes.

'Probably,' he answers softly.

'That explains it,' she smiles.

And then there is only the sound of the sea. After a while she can feel something playing gently with her hair. It could be the kitten, but she suspects it is he. She opens her eyes for a moment. Just long enough to see that he too is lying back, eyes closed, smiling. His hands. The slow and sensual language of fingertips and palms. Tell me with your hands who you are, where you come from, what you dream. Let your fingers sing. Push against my palm, with your palm, all your joy, all your pain. Leave in my hand, from your hand, an imprint of your longing, the map of your desire. She catches her breath.

'I must go,' she says.

'Are you sure?'

'Zara is waiting for me. She gets anxious if I'm gone too long.'

'Then you will miss it.'

'Miss what?'

'The chance to be dreamed by the stars.'

She drives home very slowly. She already knows that her body would respond to him. To this man who combs the beach. But what would happen to her soul? The words of the poem in the letter come back.

> To love is to bleed with longing
> to arch one's cry to the claw of the night,
> and hope is a stone
> falling, falling
> from the tongue of a dream
> through the sky.

To what are you pledging such loyalty, Camille? She asks herself. To a memory? An illusion? Or to your pain? She sighs. The only real betrayal is the one against yourself, she mutters. Are you so committed to your broken heart that you will not allow yourself any happiness; the terrain of sorrow so familiar, so comfortable, that to leave it behind would seem like defection?

She cannot untangle it.

What she likes most about this man, this free spirit who dances the tango with a rake on the sand, is that he is as different and removed from her past as only he could be. And yes, a part of her hoped to be able to lose herself in this differentness. To forget. But instead, the opposite. Instead, with each moment of intimacy, he brings with him the ghost of the other, as though carrying a wounded soldier over his shoulder. And all she can remember is the blood.

But he has healing hands, she thinks, sinking into bed later that night with Zara. Hands that save lives. Hands that bring light.

And so, come to think of it, does she.

Part II

A plant dies and is buried again
man's feet return to the terrain,
only wings evade death.

– Neruda

They eat dinner on their laps. A hearty vegetable stew with big chunks of fresh bread. The old man refills their wine glasses. Pieter shakes his head as his turn comes, but the old man fills it anyway.

'I have to drive tonight,' Pieter says.

'A little more is not going to do any harm. And anyway, tonight is a special night. Tonight Blom is home.'

Blom raises her glass and grins. Then turns to Pieter. 'Where are you going?' she asks.

'Back into Cape Town. Some of the guys from my class are getting together. I thought I'd go along.'

'That's nice,' she says. 'I love the city at night.'

'Take her with you,' the old man says.

'Would you like to?' he offers. Not what he had in mind. Unless of course Zara came along too. 'Zara? What about you? We could all go.'

Zara shakes her head.

'I'll come,' says Blom. 'Jus' give me five minutes to get ready. Soon as I'm finished dinner I'll run home.'

'Are you back for good?' he asks her in the car. She has returned in a very pretty, very short dress, with high sandals. In sitting position the dress creeps up her brown thighs.

'I hope not,' she says.

'Why?'

'Because I hate this place.'

'Prefer the Karoo?'

'Any place so long as it's not here.'

'I thought you liked it. You always seem so happy.'

'No point dropping your lip.'

'I suppose so.'

He does not press her. With Leah as the family domestic, and having grown up with Blom, he knows quite enough about her family to understand how difficult it must be for her to live here. As a child, she had no choice. But suddenly, now, it seems she has left childhood behind. Certainly her body is no longer that of a girl.

He wonders if she knows of the plans to give some land and vines to the labourers. Goiya has a fairly senior position among the labourers, and would be sure to be selected as part of the team, maybe even as the leader. He hopes so. It could mean more money for him. A sense of dignity.

Pieter's father has been in meetings all week with neighbouring wine farmers to discuss the nuts and bolts of this new scheme: how much land to give them, how much control, how much time off. He catches snippets of it in passing. His father would never discuss it with him, of course. He made that quite clear when Pieter decided to study engineering rather than viticulture. And in some ways, he feels relieved. But he cannot help hearing him droning on at endless meetings, many of which are held in their home. When he first heard of the scheme, his suspicions were raised. Something is afoot. He wouldn't want to speak for the others, but giving land away – giving *anything* away – is most unlike his father. He must be up to something. And then last night, he overheard the answer. He was lying on his bed reading, his bedroom directly above the dining room where the meeting was taking place.

'We're asking for trouble, Hermann,' said Kobus Fouché.

'Look, it's going to be a bloody mess, that's for sure,' agreed his father. 'But the money's overseas now, Kobie. The money's overseas and this is helluva good for marketing. Bloody foreigners get all bleary-eyed about that sort of thing. They'll buy the wine from the guys who are seen to be giving the darkies a share of the pie, I'm telling you.'

He took up his book again, smiled and shook his head. He might have guessed.

It takes an hour to reach Cape Town. He has always enjoyed the drive. But there are times when he wishes it weren't quite so far. His friends are meeting at the Waterfront. His friends? Not really. Friendly, yes. And funny. And necessary, in a way. But not friends for life. Not like Zara.

And yet lately he has felt something inside him changing. Shifting. A restlessness he cannot define is taking hold. A need to belong to something. Something beyond the valley and his father. Beyond the magnificent estate and the lush vegetation. A longing for something completely his. Not inherited.

He knows his parents are disappointed in him. He was expected to continue the tradition and take over the farm.

'That's what the de Goede boy is doing. And Japie du Plessis,' his father said when he told him he wanted to study electronic engineering. 'Viticulture. That's what you'll study if I'm paying for it. What's the matter with you? This farm not good enough for you? Engineering? Forget it!'

He knew better than to argue with his father. But he did not forget it. Why should he? Instead, with increased determination, he attached his straight-A report card and a letter from his teacher to a bursary application. He will never forget the elation when he learned that he had been awarded a substantial amount to cover fees and accommodation, plus a little extra to defray expenses. Or the freedom he felt when he used some of it to buy the old Mazda. Especially after his father had said he could walk to varsity for all he cared.

His mother, who'd opened the letter, had apparently boasted to every woman in her bridge club. Leah had actually chuckled when she gave him the details. 'Pieter won a scholarship, you know. Not that we wouldn't have sent him anyway. He's extraordinarily bright. Not sure where he gets it from.' And then that little laugh of hers. As though she knows something nobody else ever will.

By the time the news reached his father that evening, it was a fait accompli. 'Bloody fool,' was all Hermann Smit had to say about it, slamming the door and walking back out of the house.

He had not responded. Simply took his letter and headed for the bedroom. Closed the door and sat on his bed, reading the letter again and again. Holding it up to the light.

With the bursary money he could have rented a room closer to campus. Become part of the 'scene'. He still says he will. As soon as he finds the right place. As soon as he gets time to look. As soon as something comes up. Deep down he knows it is something else. For while the longing for beyond grows deeper each day, he cannot think of leaving Zara. How much longer Pappi will be there for her, who can tell? He seems to have lost weight recently; his wiriness now almost bordering on frailty. Besides, that is what he had promised Camille, silently, at her funeral. 'I'll look after her forever, Tannie,' he remembers whispering into the rain.

He always wished she were his mother too. The colourful scarves in her hair were like flags. Secret symbols of a far-off world, a little piece of which they had brought with them here. Worlds where children played the best games, returning at any point to capable arms and stories and food. She was so gentle. He remembers arriving at the cottage one windy afternoon. Blom and Zara were playing on the swings and had not seen him. He called out to them but the wind seemed to take his words and wrap them like a turban around his head. Or maybe Zara and Blom were just ignoring him. He decided to get their attention by cycling nonchalantly past them. But he underestimated the power of Blom's tiny calves to propel herself ever higher on the swing. With an astonished shriek her foot caught his shoulder and sent him with all his dignity flying from his bike on to the gravel. Zara had walked across, crouched down on her haunches and stared at him.

'I'll call Maman,' she said, vanishing indoors.

His left arm stung and blood oozed through his T-shirt sleeve. To cry would mean total surrender. But the pain. The humiliation! And what would his mother say if she knew he'd been here? All he could do was press his brows together as firmly as possible and suck his lips in.

Camille came from the house with a small bowl of tepid water and a cloth.

'Come, *petit*,' she said. 'Sit next to me on the steps and let me have a look.'

Slowly and carefully she cleaned the graze and dabbed on some Mercurochrome, humming to herself all the time, while Blom bounced around them and Zara stood quietly watching.

'You'll have a big bruise tomorrow,' she said. And then she pressed her thumb between his brows to ease the furrows. 'But no need to worry so. What about some juice?'

It was different when he fell at home. Usually his mother would scold him for being clumsy.

'Look where you're going, Pieter,' she would say. 'You're not a mongol.'

Then he would be sent to Leah who would take him tightly by the hand and haul him off to the bathroom, where she would wash the wound and douse it with vigour and stinging antiseptic.

On his mother's urging, his father had beaten him when he discovered he was visiting the small cottage. The sjambok's leather strips burning into him; in the bathroom mirror his back like a *braai* grill. He could not bath for two weeks, the hot water stung him so.

And each night when he climbed into bed he wished he had a dog like Laika to curl up with. He wished he lived, not here in this house with high ceilings and airy rooms where he suffocated from rigidity and structure, but there, cramped and warm in a magical realm of herb seedlings potted in old tin cans and children's drawings on the walls. A world filled with possibilities and imagination.

The beatings taught him not obedience, but how to lie. And instead of dampening his ardour to visit the cottage, it sharpened it. He persuaded Leah to cover for him.

'Yes, Merrem, I saw him. He's on his bike. He's

around.' Although she reprimanded him fiercely whenever she could.

'You want to get me fired?'

'No, Leah.'

'Then stop going over there all the time and thinking I'm going to protect you.'

But she could see in his face she was fighting a losing battle. The child was bewitched by friendship, and who could blame him, the poor little bastard?

She too had niggling feelings of doubt about the setup. She could see that Blom had flourished in just a few months. She cried less, was less demanding, was happier. But was she not allowing her child to set herself up for terrible disappointments? When the dice fell later in life, Zara would have opportunities, Blom would not. Zara might go to university. Travel back to Europe. Leaving Blom, who would probably get a job as a domestic (providing the blerry blacks didn't get there first). Whereas if she played with her own kind, she might not enjoy it as much now, but later on she'd be more content. Marry a local boy. Have her own family.

And then Pieter. Was it a good idea for them to get too close? She clenches her jaw. Is *that* the reason the pig beat the daylights out of him when they found he'd been playing over there? Bastard. Was it really Zara they were keeping him from? Or Blom? She feels with her tongue for the ridge in the gap between her teeth and the comfort of its faintly metallic taste. Runs a rough hand over the lump on her head. Had she bumped herself, or was that Goiya? It is hard to keep track, these days.

The crowd sit outside on bucket chairs, among gulls and boats and legs and laughter. It is a warm evening. Salt-infused.

'This is Blom,' he says.

There are murmurs of greetings. As they find themselves seats, one or two of the crowd turn to look at Blom again.

'What can I get you?' a boy called Jaco asks them on his way to the bar.

'A beer,' he says. He would prefer wine.

'A Coke,' says Blom. '*Ag nee, a glassie wyn.*' She turns to the person next to her and grins.

'Glad you made it, Piet,' says one of the guys on the other side of the table. 'What did you make of today's test?'

When he turns around she is chatting effortlessly. He starts to relax.

As the evening progresses, classmates he has never spoken to wander over to him to chat. At first he cannot understand it. Why all of a sudden? They've had all year to befriend him, why now? But after catching a few of their stolen glances at Blom, he starts to understand and a strange warm feeling creeps through him. He sits up straight in his chair, stretches his shoulders back and orders another beer. The glow of the lamps like honey on the water.

'Hey, Piet? What are you and Blom doing on Saturday? We're having a *braai*, why don't you join us?'

On the drive home they slip into a comfortable silence. Now and again her fresh smell. Something crushed. A spice. His face slightly tilted as he looks across at her now and then, watching her stare out into the night, softly singing. He wonders where she is. And with whom.

'How do you feel about Saturday? The *braai*?' he asks when they reach the valley.

'I love the city,' she says, half to herself. 'Yes. Let's go.'

Later, as the night spins slowly away from itself, the stillness in the valley is a mirror of the sky. He falls asleep, his mind a swirl. Dreams of a spiral staircase. He is stuck on a landing and must choose whether to go up or down. He has no idea where either direction will lead. Further down the road, in quarters where the sour smell of stale alcohol is the only reminder of the violence a few hours before, Blom too sighs in her sleep. She dreams she is sitting on Table Mountain at night, the fairy lights of the city below her and a red bicycle lying at her side.

TWENTY

FRANK ROSEN HANGS up the telephone, stubs out his Gauloise and settles down to read the paper once again. He notices a spelling mistake in the third line of his art review column. Swears, then grins, showing brown nicotine stains on his teeth. He planned to write that the artist's Impressionist style suggests the faintest influence of Monet. But in print, a 'y' has replaced the 't', making it 'Money' instead. 'The artist's Impressionist style suggests the faintest influence of Money.' How Freudian. And so often the case these days; there seems to be an infinite well of cleverly marketed crap. He sniffs and lights another Gauloise. At least his pending retirement, after what seems a lifetime of judging and weighing the value of art, will provide him with a complete change. He will spend more time at home tending his tomatoes and fixing the house. He will have some of his favourite paintings reframed, and will bother to attend only the exhibitions of those painters he admires and respects. Good painters unencumbered by the undulating challenges of their egos. 'Isn't that right, Fellini?' He strokes the triangular head of the oriental black cat who is settling himself down on the main section of the newspaper in the sun. 'What do you say?'

Fellini flicks his tail.

Maybe he wouldn't be feeling quite so acid had he not just spoken to Maria. That egregious social climber has invited him to another of her pretentious exhibitions, the purpose of which, no doubt, will be to punt her egotistical companion's latest artistic aspirations.

Not that the man is without talent. But unfortunately the House of Art has too many mansions, offering space to too many squatters and exploiters. Their driving force the measles of red spots at an exhibition. And an increasingly gullible public, uneducated in art, with ever more money to spend. A coterie of sycophants. Where Jake Coleman fits into all this, Frank cannot say. There is such a fine line between the genuine and the fake, the authenticity of passion and the whirlpool of spin and marketing and gimmicks. Jake has had his moments, his flashes of brilliance, no doubt about that. But not for a very long time now.

He sniffs, then draws on the Gauloise. Turns to the cat again. 'Ah, Fellini . . . it seems the nouveaux riches have inherited the earth. And art – or no, wait, *creativity* – is replacing tennis parties as the favoured hobby of this little troop of bored bourgeois plutocrats.'

Still, he reasons, he can always use this exhibition to his own advantage. Several overseas art publications have been pestering him for an article; something on new trends in art at the southern tip of Africa. Hopefully, there will be some students 'of colour' in the mix. Which means he could comment on the exhibition and include something with an ethnic flavour. He finds it wryly amusing that African ethnicity has such exotic appeal and nobility. Especially if it is an artist who has survived the Struggle. And he could always use the same article for his column in the local papers. That would save him time and effort. And it would be one article closer to freedom.

Maria hangs up the phone and pauses. Frank is always so unfriendly and negative. Often downright unpleasant if it comes down to it. He should be grateful to her. Not rude. Without people like her he wouldn't have a job! She lights a cigarette and phones the coffee shop next door to ask them to deliver a latte and a fruit tartlet. She'll go to gym later. She'll work it off.

Personally, she doesn't know why people hold Frank Rosen's opinion in such regard. He's acerbic and uncouth. One would think he'd need some finesse for a job such as his, but if he does have any, he certainly doesn't seem to let on. Perhaps it's because he's been with the papers so long? she muses. A dirty old hack who knows how to manipulate himself into a cushy job. He's never even bought a single painting from her.

She walks outside to see whether the latte is on its way. Browses through the extravagant holidays on offer in the window of the travel agency on her left. Perhaps she could persuade Jake to take a trip. She'd love to go on a cruise. Something special. Perhaps *then* things might improve between them.

Just then, a jackhammer starts up. They appear to be fixing a pothole. She moves inside as her drink arrives, the noise gnawing at her skull. She picks up the latest copy of *Odyssey* magazine and flicks through an article on feng shui. Perhaps she could get a consultant in, not only to the shop but to her home as well. That may help to shift the bad energy. Her eye catches an advertisement in the corner of the page: *Tarot readings. Constantia.* She circles it with a pen. Now that would be an interesting experience. She has only been once before, and found it astonishingly accurate. Not a bad idea to see whether her instincts are on track. She is a firm believer in trusting one's instincts. But has often wondered where instinct ends and paranoia begins. Can the shadow and the higher self dance cheek to cheek? Do we, in fact, create the situations we most fear? Or simply know in advance how something will end?

The door sensor rings. She leaves her pen inside the magazine to mark her place, and looks up. She recognises the Hungarian potter.

'Mátyás! What a surprise. What are you doing here?'

'I've been driving and driving. I couldn't find you,' he beams.

'Do we have a meeting?' she says.

'I thought we did,' he scratches his blond head. 'Am I wrong again?'

'We were supposed to have one last week. When I didn't see you, I thought perhaps you couldn't make it.'

'Ah. So I'm a week late. That's okay.' He sits down in front of her, and delves into a plastic bag. 'Here, I brought you this.' From the bag he produces a potted cactus. 'Isn't he beautiful?' he grins.

'Well, yes. Yes! Stunning. Nobody has ever given me a cactus before.'

'This is what I was thinking. So, I am the first. That's beautiful.'

'Would you like some coffee, Mátyás? Can I order you a latte, a cappuccino, an espresso? And what about a fruit tartlet? The people next door make the most ambrosial food.'

'Only if you have some too.' He is still smiling.

'Oh, I've just had. But . . . okay. It's not every day we get together.'

She is suddenly delighted to see him. His simple affection is contagious. A celebration.

'I also brought you these,' he says. And from the bag he produces some exquisite pottery tea bowls.

'Oh, Mátyás. I *love* those. Will you leave them with me for the shop? Let's see if we can make you rich?'

'Rich? Why not? It will be a brand new experience for me.' The laughter lines deepen around his eyes.

'Then we must try! I'd like to make you rich for the first time.'

'Ah, I like first times,' he says.

She cannot know that in a valley near a rock pool, her partner has just made love to a woman half her age. And that at this moment he is watching the young woman who lies quietly alongside him, staring up at a darkening sky. Perhaps if he waits long enough, he will make sense of her contradictions, he thinks. Her sensuality and her silence. Find some pattern in her behaviour. A rhythm. The wind runs fingers through the leaves. It is getting cold. A large raindrop breaks on to her forehead.

She is the rain cycle, he muses. The swollen wave as it rises to lick the moon. The dew on a leaf, pulling, pulling, tugged by a force outside itself until it breaks free, transformed into one cloud, then the next, arched against eternity. And as the lightning tears the landscape, she gives herself away with the rain, falling first in hard steady beats, subsiding later into gentle pulses. At the heart of each cycle, an impenetrable desolation.

He must just be patient, he tells himself. It will come, the light.

TWENTY-ONE

FOR PIETER, THE engineering course is sometimes an uncomfortably masculine affair. Mechanical. Full of angles. The lecturers progress through the course systematically and with meticulous precision. He must concentrate. He cannot afford to miss anything. He cannot afford to fail. And yet this has become difficult of late. Before he can stop himself, a thought has enticed him and pulled him all the way down its path; by the time he realises that he has missed half the lecture.

During coffee breaks the students thaw in the sun. They seem to include him more since the evening at the Waterfront.

'Are you coming over on Saturday night?' Jaco asks.

'Sure,' says Pieter.

'With Blom?' Jaco enquires. Is he reading his mind?

'Ja,' he says, trying to sound careless. 'Sure.'

The feelings collide; on the one hand he enjoys the new respect this perception has afforded him. And on the other, he feels annoyed by their interest in her. In some ways Blom is like family. He's known her almost all his life. It's inappropriate for callow engineering students to be noticing her so obviously. They must leave her alone.

But mostly there is a lightness in him, a sweetness to living, that he has not known before. A strange relief.

Since he was five years old he has known two things: that there is only Zara. And that he would never have her. And in some ways that has not changed. Cannot change. He is defined by these two simple facts. And yet he feels as though he is on holiday from the weight of that knowledge.

Late that afternoon he stops at the labourers' cottages. Leah is wringing out some washing. She looks at him questioningly, her face twisting with every squeeze.

'Hello, Leah,' he says. After all these years he is still wary of her.

'Ja?' she replies.

'I'm looking for Blom.'

'Ja, so?'

'Well, is she here?'

'Maybe.'

Hearing his voice, Blom appears at the door.

'Hi,' she grins.

'Feel like a walk?' he says suddenly, trying his best to ignore Leah's glare. 'It's such a beautiful evening.'

'I'll just get my jas,' she says. 'Wait.'

'Your mother doesn't look impressed,' he says as they proceed down the dust road.

'Ja, I dunno what's her problem,' says Blom. 'Never mind.'

'Are you sure?' He asks quietly. He is never certain what Blom must endure from her parents. He would hate for them to take it out on her.

'Ja, relax, man!' She gives a grin and a playful slap on the arm. 'Now tell me about the party.'

The party begins as a braai. Pieter has brought meat for both himself and Blom. He went to the supermarket that morning. Spent a good while at the meat counter, wondering what she would prefer. In the end he decided to err on the side of plenty: sosaties, wors, chicken breasts and steaks. Other people could always benefit from what they couldn't manage to eat themselves. When he put the meat in the fridge at home, his father raised his bushy eyebrows.

'Somebody obviously has too much money to spend. What do you think you're feeding, a bloody army?'

'It's my money, Pa,' he said.

He has also taken a bottle of good white wine from the cellar. Hidden it in a cooler bag under his sweaters, and smuggled it out of the house in a rucksack. His father watches him leave, a thick scowl smeared across his face.

By the time they arrive the music and voices and laughter are already very loud. They are playing grunge rock. Pearl Jam. Plastic bowls of chips and saucers of oily peanuts adorn the tables and a large bucket of yellow punch with the odd chunk of fruit is spilt with gusto into various glasses. He tries to appear relaxed, nodding his head in time to the music and smiling. Smacks back some of the oversweet punch with Blom before opening the wine. But still he feels self-conscious. Everybody must know it's just an act. One or two people sing along with Pearl Jam. Already some people are dancing. He envies their abandon. Their complete surrender to the music. Blom too moves effortlessly with the rhythm. Her narrow hips swaying, her pretty shoulders moving forward and back. It reminds him of when he first saw her all those years ago, with Zara, practising for their concert. Even then he realised that some people were born to dance with flair and fire. He wishes he could have been one of them. He drinks his wine as quickly as he can and tops up his glass. For reasons beyond him, it is not having the effect he desired. Instead of becoming more relaxed he is starting to feel more and more isolated, instead of numbing the senses it seems to be making them more acute.

Right before his eyes, Jaco asks Blom to dance.

'Later,' says Blom. He could kiss her.

'Come,' she says, taking his hand. 'Let's have something to eat.'

After they have eaten, he stands up bravely. He must ask her to dance, there is no way around it. If he doesn't, somebody else will, that's for sure, and then he will be left on his own all night. Worse still, they will think she has left him for someone else!

'Shall we dance?' He tries to look careless, even though he has no clue what he will do with his long, uncoordinated legs.

'Ja,' she says. 'Good idea.'

To begin with he finds that the less he moves, the better. He just shuffles his shoulders a little this way, then that. His best bet is to mirror Blom, to copy her as best he can. On no account must he reveal how hard he is concentrating. He must feign nonchalance at all costs. In spite of his efforts, Blom quickly comes to the rescue, taking his arms and lightly guiding him. He follows her lead, trying one or two steps, tentatively at first, and repeats them over and again, first in his mind, and then in his body. Not bad. It's a bit like working out a mathematical formula. Not too bad at all. His stiffness starts to dissolve, and soon the music starts creeping into him. Soon he finds himself imagining he must look all right. He is dancing. Really dancing! Just like the others. Every now and again he even mouths the words of the song.

When she eventually drags him off the dance floor for a rest she is laughing.

'Haai! You naughty boy, you never told me you liked dancing so much.'

She never said he was any good, mind you. But he is too happy to care. People seem to be smiling at him, and he smiles back, feeling the collective joy. He puts his arm around Blom and feels the light warmth of her smooth arm against his back in return.

The evening falls away from them all too soon. There is more dancing, more wine, somebody passes a joint around, and driving home in the car, both sing. When he stalls the car outside the Septembers' cottage they both start to giggle.

He gets out of the car with her.

'Haai! What are you doing?'

'I don't know. I don't want to go home yet,' he says. 'It's boring.'

She stifles a chuckle. 'Well, you can't stay here.' Quite suddenly she looks worried.

'I know. Shall we go to the dam?'

In the still conspiracy of the night they fall silent. When they reach the dam he stops and looks up at the moon, ice-white tonight, a giant street lamp for all the world, and wonders what he must look like from up there: a young man peering upwards, balanced precariously at the edge of his universe, at the very point in his life when the future is peeling away from the past, and the present is so dense that he hardly dares to breathe. He turns to Blom and releases her small hand.

'The bushes look like they're moving,' she says.

'I don't want to look at the bushes. I want to look at you.' He feels the contours of her face with his hands. Then very tentatively he drops his mouth on to hers. In the cool of the night the soft warmth of this action makes him catch his breath, and the evening is suddenly seamed with magic. 'Thank you,' he whispers.

They walk back to the cottages very slowly. When he finally drives away she pauses a while at the front door before meticulously turning the handle and creeping in. Something is moving in the shadows.

'Who's there?' she whispers.

No reply. 'Who's there?' she repeats. 'Mommy?'

'Wat?'

'Where's Pa?'

'He's passed out next door. What else is new?'

'Are you okay?'

Again no reply.

'Are you okay, Mommy?' Her mother's silence frightens her.

'Has he hit you, Mommy? Are you okay? Tell me!'

She hears a sniff. 'No. He didn't hit me. This time it's you.'

'*Me?* What've I done?'

'Blom, I'm asking you once. Please don't see that boy again.'

'Pieter? Pieter's not *that boy*. He's Pieter. He's like your son, how can you call him *that boy*?'

'Don't make me ask you again, Blom. I'm asking you now.'

'Well, you can't expect me to listen unless you have a fokken good reason.' She is growing angry. Has her mother been drinking?

'Okay, girl, you asked for it.' Leah smooths her hands on her lap and takes a deep breath. 'When that fat pig had his way with you, and we sent you off quickly to the Karoo?'

'Ja.'

'Well, you were lucky.'

'I didn't feel very lucky. What do you mean?'

'I was also pretty once, you know. I didn't always look like this. And when I was your age, it was me.'

'He raped you too?'

'Not once. Not twice. A lot of times.' Leah starts to heave.

'Jesus,' whispers Blom, putting her arm awkwardly around her mother. 'It's all right, Mommy,' she says. 'Come now.'

As her mother's sobs subside, she asks, more to herself than Leah, 'But what made you think about it all now? Pieter is not like his father. We all know that.'

In the dark she can just see her mother lift her head and face her. In the dark is where her answer belongs.

'He is your father too.'

Before his son has even climbed out of the car, Hermann Smit has pulled him out by the arm and sunk his knuckles into the boy's gut.

'Think I brought you up to fuck Hotnots?' he hisses.

He does not expect the boy's reaction. Sees him wrench a fencepost free and watches in immobilised horror as the knockout whack fuelled by a lifetime of rage knocks him senseless against the wall.

'That's the last time, Pa,' he says, before getting back into the car and driving away.

TWENTY-TWO

To AVOID MARIA he stays in his studio. Some of the time he spends paging through art journals, although he never seems to find the articles he's looking for. When he does, he becomes irritated with them, questioning why he ever considered them to be of any value at all. Some of the time he spends preparing lectures, although the content seems fragmented to him. He cannot ever seem to find the one connecting thread that ties a brilliant lecture together. And some of the time he paints. The canvas is coming along tortuously. He has redone parts of it – certain parts will not be resolved – and he has even begun dreaming about it at night, waking in a panic, confused and angry.

That is when he can sleep. Mostly, he lies awake night after night, falling asleep only when the birds begin the business of their day. Then often he wakes a short while later, gripped with irrational fear. Sometimes of insanity, sometimes death, sometimes both. *Why is he pursuing her? Is he mad? Will he ever paint again? What if Maria leaves him? Who is Pieter? Why does all this affect him so much? Is he dying?* He gives up coffee in a vague attempt to soothe a heartbeat speeding out of control.

And then he misses his appointment with the Dutch visitors. Trudy had sent him an e-mail reminder, which he received the previous day; he had even written it into his Filofax. But after a night of tossing and turning, he longs to have the house to himself, to sleep a little, have a relaxed breakfast and ease slowly into the day. He knows he doesn't really have to be in until later, with students working on their exhibition submissions. He has already asked Maria to disconnect the telephone. And the appointment with the Dutch people sails cleanly out of his head.

When he switches on his cellphone at ten o'clock, there are three strained messages from Trudy; the last indicating that the Dutch men had gone. They had not left a number. They said if they still needed him at all they might call.

He drives to the school. Only three more days to the exhibition. The press has been alerted; already there are write-ups, small articles in the arts sections of various papers. He switches on the radio to catch the tail end of a talk show. The host ending off with ' . . . not to be missed. Jake Coleman will be releasing a new work. The first in some time. A breakthrough, his agent says. That, plus all the newest talent on the block. See you there!' A breakthrough? Sometimes he hates Maria. Is this revenge? He trudges into the school. The students don't need this kind of pressure either. It's ludicrous.

The simple frame Zara has made for her painting is remarkably effective. So much so that the rest of the class take silent note. He watches them pretend to walk idly past, try to catch a glimpse, then become pensive. She ignores them and him, although now and again he notices her lips moving. He has established that she is not in fact talking to herself as he originally thought. She is singing.

He has a headache. The exhibition is making him ill.

What if he doesn't have anything to show? It has the students worried too. He can tell by their silence. They seem tired and strained. It can't be easy for them either, poor kids. This is their first real opportunity. All of them desperate not to blow it. Only Zara is unconcerned. It is not natural.

'Here is my painting,' she says, dropping a big, framed canvas board off in his office and turning to leave.

'Wait.'

She stops.

'Zara, you have to stop doing your own thing all the time.'

Silence.

'You put me in a very difficult position. I don't want to chastise you. But I haven't even seen your painting. That's not how we work here.'

'See it now.'

'That's not the point. What if it's not right? Not good enough? Then what?'

She shrugs. He feels the blood flood his face.

'You can't just shrug it off. Either you want to be a student like everyone else, or you don't.' He stops. He can't believe he is shouting

She stares at him.

What a stupid thing to say. Stupid! What if she really decided to leave? Why give her a way out like that?

'Okay, let's take a look at the painting,' he says. He tries to smile. To breathe.

She props it up against the wall.

'Hmmm,' he mumbles. Then, 'Jesus.'

She waits. After a short while she says, 'Can I go now?'

He ignores her, staring at the painting. Her first self-portrait. In it, her eyes are closed, her lips are parted. Black blood drips from her mouth.'

'Well, same old cheerful theme, I see. Macabre as ever.'

But it is brilliant. It makes him want to retch.

'It's called *Innocence*,' she says.

'Jesus,' he mutters, 'how do you work that one out? There's black blood dripping from her jowls, for Chrissake. It looks satanic!'

'Innocence is black. Not white.'

'Huh?'

'White is a negation. It is not a colour, only a reflection. It does not exist. Within black, there is every colour. What you call innocence is simply a state of unknowing. Naivety. What I call innocence embraces all of life's colours, and celebrates it.'

'Well, if you call this a celebration, then I don't know.'

She is silent again. He sighs.

'It's very good, Zara.'

'May I go now?' she asks again.

'I suppose so.' Then, 'Zara, wait. The opening. It's at seven on Saturday night. I'll see you there.'

When he looks up she is gone. He takes one further glance at the painting, before turning it to face the wall and sinking into his chair.

There is nothing he can teach this girl. Where the fuck does talent like this come from? And why does he have to have it shoved down his throat now?

Some students have already finished their pieces. Some of them have even sent their work off for framing and are enjoying a day or so of respite, strolling around and smoking while their fellow students frown and fret over the wisdom of last-minute alterations.

'When does one know if it's finished?' they agonise.

'When it starts to sing,' says Jake. 'Matisse talks about painting until the hand sings.'

But mostly there is an air of unspoken anticipation. And a new cohesion in the class. A sense of joint focus and quiet victory over their own dark vulnerabilities. After the exhibition there is only one more week left of term, before they have a month's break. They deserve their holiday.

He envies them.

Last night he worked into the early hours of the morning. But still his painting remains unresolved. If he is going to stand any chance of making this ridiculous deadline, he will need to apply himself completely for the next three days. He arranges to meet students for an hour each day, for questions, to soothe their agitation, setting aside Friday afternoon for last-minute arrangements, and leaves Trudy in charge.

Maria cannot reach him on the telephone; he has disconnected it. And when she returns in the afternoon she dares not disturb him. When she knocks on the door at seven to ask if he wants dinner, she finds him not painting, but pacing. He wants his dinner there. He does not wish to be disturbed.

She does not know when he sleeps. But she knows better than to ask. Besides, she too is apprehensive. This is the first time she has involved Jake's students. The first time she is asserting herself at the school. On no account can she allow the smallest thing to go wrong. Her position must be made clear, in the most professional manner possible. It is the dignified way to handle matters. She also feels sure that if there is something to uncover, this is the evening it will be revealed.

She has started losing weight. She knows it is sheer nervous tension that is agitating her metabolism. An underlying fear that has found its way, like a shadow, into everything she thinks or does. She feels sure that talking to a friend about it may help. But that is out of the question, of course. If Cecily, Lily, or *any* of that circle of friends, were to believe that she and Jake were having problems, she would become gossip fodder at every conclave of nodding, knowing heads. She needs someone safer. A container. Suddenly, Mátyás's tea bowls, simple and womb-like, spring to mind. Instinctively, she lifts the phone.

A few hours later she is sitting at a heavy wooden kitchen table in a kitchen in Mátyás's A-frame house in Glencairn. The wooden house is built against the cliff. Birds gather and scatter where he has thrown crumbs on a patch of green lawn in front. Bags of clay are stacked against a wall. While he brews a fresh pot of coffee, she runs her fingertips along the table surface, lifts them and examines them. Red dust. Clay. He hands her the rich, steaming beverage in a pottery mug.

'You make these?' she asks.

'Of course.'

He does not ask why she is there. And she does not tell him. They simply drink coffee and discuss tea bowls.

'I was wondering,' she says, rising to leave. 'I'm having an exhibition at the gallery. Some students from Jake's school. I would love to show some of your tea bowls too?'

'I'm flattered,' he says.

'Would you come?'

He begins to decline, but stops. There is something in her face, something intense and raw that makes him change his mind.

'Yes,' he says. 'I'll come. Thank you.'

'Thank *you*,' she answers.

At 4 a.m. on the morning of the exhibition Jake crawls onto the bed. He still has paint on his hands and a smear on his cheek and is too tired even to pull back the covers on his side. But he is satisfied at last. Now he will sleep and tomorrow he will have 'the painting' for the exhibition.

It is quite different from his usual style. Far more detailed. Obscure. Called *Man-Rope* it depicts a man unnaturally contorted, limbs unnaturally threaded and stretched across an abyss. On the one side, Bosch-like demons with oversized heads and enormous mouths. On the other, if you look carefully, the image of a woman, long-limbed and naked, holding a bowl of fruit. The inspiration came from Nietzsche. From *Thus Spake Zarathustra*. Zara. Thustra.

Man is a rope linking beast and superman – a rope across a chasm . . . What is great about man is that he is a bridge and not an end; what can be loved in man is that he is a crossing over and a passing below.

As he sleeps in the splendour of his home and the comfort of a job well done, Zara is wakened by the smallest of whines in her cottage. 'What is it, Laika?' she whispers. The dog is sitting in the entrance to the alcove where she sleeps. The cottage is quiet except for the hum of the fridge. As she turns over to sleep, the dog whines again. 'Come, Laika. Come to bed.' When the old dog does not move she rises and walks into the living area, looks out of the window. 'There's nobody there. It's fine.'

Pappi must be awake, she cannot hear him snoring. She tilts her head round his door. 'Everything okay, Pappi?' In the faint light she can just see his outline; he is lying on his back. The blanket has fallen off him, he must be cold. She tiptoes inside. Lifts the blanket from the floor and covers him. He does not wake. She sits softly beside him and watches him for a few moments while Laika whines. He is not snoring. Not moving. She strokes his forehead. He is so still. As she leans across him to hear if he is breathing, she slowly starts to understand that his tired blue eyes will not open again. 'Pappi,' she whispers, stroking his hand, watching him for some time. ' "Only wings evade death". Neruda. Remember?'

In the morning she feeds Laika very early.

'We must bury him today,' she tells him. 'But first we must tell Pieter and Blom. Before they go out.'

The two head off first to the Smits' farm. This is the first time that Zara has ever walked up their pathway to the big wooden door with the brass knocker.

'Is Pieter here?' she asks Mrs Smit.

'No.' Mrs Smit seems angry. Her top lip is tight and pale. 'He doesn't live here any more.' And then she closes the door.

They walk back past their home and on to the labourers' cottages. Small children in black-and-white school uniforms are bobbing around the brick structures, and women are leaving for work. When she reaches the end of the row, she knocks at the door of the Septembers' cottage. No answer. Only after she has knocked again does someone open the door. Goiya. With a long gash on his cheek.

'Is Blom here?' she asks.

'Blom's gone, my lady,' says Goiya.

'When will she be back?'

'She's not coming back. Her mother says she's gone for good.'

Zara stares at him.

'Is Leah here?'

'No, she left for work. I'm waiting to go to the clinic.'

'My grandfather died this morning. I need to bury him.'

The bony Coloured man looks at her with large bloodshot eyes and hollow cheeks. 'Wait,' he says, after some time. 'I'll come.'

There is a plot of land that labourers have been given to bury their families. Plastic flowers and decorations adorn each grave with a cheerfulness that belies the sadness of each passing. After they have found an empty spot, one with enough shade, enough light, Goiya tells her to go home. This is a man's business. He needs to obtain permission for the burial. Ask Leah to phone the undertakers. He also needs to dig the grave.

Back at the cottage, she struggles to sit still. The racing section of the newspaper lies curled on the table, with Pappi's pipe and a half-full packet of tobacco. She folds the newspaper. Then walks to her bedroom and lifts the brown suitcase off the top of the wardrobe, brings it through to the living area and unclips it. She places the newspaper inside it, with the pumpkin folder, stopping to note the date – the 13th of the month – before lifting the tobacco to her nose, then placing that inside the suitcase too. Then she walks into his room where he lies, now smooth and serene.

'Number thirteen came in for you again, Pappi,' she says with a small smile. 'At last, huh?'

She takes the tatty book of Neruda poems from his side table. That too is placed inside the suitcase. A longing to preserve the texture of his life. For remembering.

A while later, a man arrives to take the body away.

'We'll bring it back, Miss,' the driver assures her. 'Please fill in these forms.'

Goiya returns later that afternoon, followed by two labourers. Just then the hearse crawls up the gravel driveway. He has a quick word with the driver, and the car pulls away again for the graveyard.

Once there, he whistles through the gap in his teeth, jerking his head in the direction of the black car. The two labourers quickly make their way to the vehicle. They ease the simple knotty-pine coffin slowly out into the daylight and carry it carefully to the freshly dug grave. There it will lie, among many others, in this humble place; a strange combination of raw red earth, gravestones and bright fake flowers.

The funeral is over in minutes. Goiya has asked an old Coloured man to read a prayer. This he does very slowly, articulating each word as though his own salvation depends upon it. Leah is there too, her head covered with an old lace scarf, holding a small posy of flowers. She does not look up at anybody. Stands staring at the grave as though in it she can see another world.

'Blom would have liked to be here,' she says quietly. 'She loved the old bugger.'

Goiya stands alongside her, thin and intent, wearing his old red cap. The two labourers also stay to pay respects, leaning forward and bobbing every now and again. After the prayer, on Goiya's command, they pick up their spades and fill the grave. Leah throws her posy in with the coffin. Zara drops to her haunches and holds the dog. When they empty the last spadeful of earth to seal up the fissure, Laika immediately breaks free, jumps onto the freshly turned soil and starts frantically digging.

'Come, Laika,' says Zara. 'We're going home now.' But the dog will not budge.

'Come *on*, Laika,' she repeats, trying to pull him at first, before giving up.

'Here, this for you,' Leah says, handing Zara a scrap of paper with a number on it. 'Pieter. His telephone. He was looking for Blom. This is where he stay now. In town.'

'And Blom?' Zara asks.

'God knows. The Karoo? I'm waiting for my sister to write back from there.'

When she looks across at Goiya, he is blowing his nose and clearing his throat, his red eyes redder than before. 'Time for a dop,' he says under his breath.

*

They hold elegant glasses at waist level and gabble and poke their necks forward towards the paintings and squint. His students stand in small groups or lean against the wall and watch. They avoid the eyes of the public, nervous in case people think they are paying too much attention to their own paintings.

Maria has done a sterling job. The lighting is perfect. The placing of each painting ideal. She has Vivaldi's *Four Seasons* playing in the background. And excellent bubbly to ease and enthuse the guests.

Zara's painting is against the back wall. His painting is with two others at the entrance, visible from the foyer where people are queuing for programmes. It is now half an hour into the evening, and Zara has not yet arrived. He drains his glass and replaces it from a tray carried by a spotty teenager in a tuxedo. Then starts to navigate the obligatory mingle.

'Good evening, Frank,' he says a little too brightly. How he despises Frank Rosen. Vindictive son of a bitch.

'Hello,' says Frank, brushing past him. You'd think he could clean himself a little for a function like this. The man has no respect. He looks like a mechanic. Jake moves on. Oh God. Patrick Le Roux. The overbearing gynaecologist. How do women *cope* with him? Let alone allow him to rummage around their bodies.

'Hello, Patrick,' he says.

'Sport! Marvellous show you have here. Great talent. You'll be out of a job soon if you have too many more of these soirées.' He roars with laughter. Slaps him on the back, spilling champagne.

'Nice to see you,' says Jake, moving away. A caramel hand touches him softly on the sleeve. Lily. Serene as ever.

'But Jake,' she says, 'I haven't seen anything of yours. I thought there was going to be at least one?'

'There is. In front.'

'Oh, I'm sorry. I must have missed it.'

He is sure he can hear Frank Rosen snigger as he walks by.

'You may not have recognised my style immediately,' he says. 'This one's a little different.'

The big Hungarian potter is here too. Jake finds him in front of Zara's painting, staring. He pats him on the back. Extends his hand.

'Mátyás. Good to see you. I'm glad Maria invited you.'

'Yes, hello.' Mátyás smiles, but without his usual conviction. It is Zara's painting that engages him. Jake can sense it. He feels his stomach contract.

Zara is still not here. He glances at the door. He should be used to it by now. The girl does exactly as she pleases. Then quite suddenly he sees her in his mind's eye, her skin in the sun, her nipples tight against his tongue, the sweet fit of her sex as he moves inside her, her thighs still wet from their swim. Maybe something happened.

'Jake!' This is the second time Maria has called him. 'Where are you? I'm talking to you.'

Trudy, holding a tray of neat, triangular sandwiches, steals a look as she passes. Maria deliberately takes his hand.

'Come. I want to show you how well it's going so far.'

She leads him to the table in the corner and, continuing to hold his hand, shows him a list of all the paintings, where she has marked with an 'S' the ones sold.

'Have you seen all the red stickers? Isn't it wonderful?'

He notices that his painting has not been sold yet; takes a quick breath. Must be the price. It was obviously, naturally, ten times more expensive than anything else on exhibition. That does make folk think twice. He shakes his hand free from Maria and scours the list. Many of the students have sold; they'll be overjoyed. Zara too.

'Who bought it?'

'Which one?' she asks.

'The self-portrait. Pascal.'

'Frank. Can you believe it? Frank, in all the time I've known him, has never bought a single painting from me. It's fabulous!'

'Bastard,' says Jake through his teeth, feeling any enthusiasm drain from him like soapy water from a dirt-rimmed bath. 'What is there to drink, Maria?'

'Bubbly? Let me catch the steward.'

'No, I'm tired of it. Surely there's something else?'

'Jake! Maria! Isn't it wonderful?'

'Cecily,' says Jake, monotone.

'I must have it of course,' she says.

'Of course you must,' says Maria. 'Which one?'

'I can't believe you're asking me that! Jake's of course. It's marvellous.'

'Yes, it is fabulous, isn't it? Do you hear that, Jake?' She threads her hand through his arm, perusing the crowd to see who notices. One or two students smile politely at her.

'Cecily's buying your painting.' A big 'S' gets added to the list in a fat black felt tip.

'Glad you like it,' he clips. Then he turns to Maria. 'Maria, I know this is bad form, but I think I'm ill. I'm going home.'

Before she can argue he walks out into the night. Maria watches as Trudy briskly crosses the room, sets the tray of sandwiches down on the counter and in her stylish heels heads for the door in his wake.

Cecily is hovering around her like a hornet, waving a cheque.

'I'll leave this with you now and pick it up later in the week.' Maria takes the cheque automatically, but has not heard a word.

The group suddenly seems so noisy. Must be the alcohol. Such a din. She sits down behind her desk. Stares long and hard at the list of paintings without seeing anything. Then lights a cigarette and gets up again, making her way over to the window. She can see them. She can see it all. Jake standing next to his car, his arms around Trudy who has her hands over her eyes. Probably crying. She takes a long drag from her cigarette and moves away.

Some of the students are leaving. Those with the little red dot the size of a fingertip next to their painting make a special effort to say goodbye to her.

'Thanks, Miss.' A boy and a girl smile and nod their bandanna-clad heads.

'It's a pleasure,' she says. 'Did you enjoy it?'

'Yes, it was rad,' says the boy. 'Totally.'

'Way cool,' smiles the girl. 'When do we, like, get the money?'

'I'll arrange that with Dr Coleman,' she says. 'Probably next week.'

'Cool,' says the girl. 'Later.' The two lift their hands stiffly in a waist-level wave, nod their heads once again and leave.

She looks at her watch. Eight thirty. It suddenly feels like the longest night of her life.

'We're leaving now, Maria,' says Lily, kissing her on the cheek. 'Thanks so much for inviting us. Very interesting. Such talent.'

'Off to dinner,' says Patrick with a nonsensical wink.

'Where is Jake?' asks Lily.

'Oh, he had to help someone with their car,' she says.

'Is this a new line for him then?' says Patrick, exploding with mirth. 'Car maintenance?'

'Let's go,' says Lily, guiding him firmly through the door.

What had she hoped? That Jake would fight off his secretary with declarations of love and commitment to herself? Deep down she has always known that she had two chances of that happening: fat and slim.

Once the last person has left, she starts to tidy up. There will be someone coming in the morning to do it. But tonight she is in no hurry to go home. She wishes she never needed to go there again. Just one more night. Then where? A hotel? Oh, please no. She has had her fill of hollow hotel rooms from her import/export days. She needs something warmer than that. Cecily? No, no. Not any of them, come to think of it. Jake has always referred to her friends as 'superficial stereotypes', and she has always instinctively defended them. 'They're happy, Jake,' she would say. 'We need more people like them.' Of course they were happy, she sees now. Being a stereotype is their highest aspiration. In their opinion, they have arrived. They have money, status and exquisite taste. She gives a little snort. Their 'taste' simply a mishmash of all that is fashionable at the time. They are clichés, every one of them. Except Mátyás. No wonder he wasn't quite himself this evening. No wonder he left very suddenly. He probably also realised that he didn't belong. She will call him in the morning. He will help her, she feels sure. How strange that this unlikely man – this man whom a few months ago she would never have dreamed of considering a member of her 'tribe' – should be the one she turns to now. She stacks the champagne glasses in their crates and begins to sweep. Once that is finished she sits down and writes out the name of each young artist, and what is owing to them. Then pulls out her chequebook and carefully writes each one a cheque, slides it into an envelope, writes a name on the front and closes it. This done, she closes the windows, flicks off the lights and makes her way to her car. She drives home slowly. There is an accident on the highway, sirens, noise, but she sticks to the left-hand lane staring straight ahead and eventually crawls up the driveway. She hopes he is asleep.

What a waste of ten years.

He is not asleep. He is drunk.

'Fucking imbeciles,' he slurs as she walks in. She goes past him and into the bathroom where she runs a bath.

'Stupid fucking idiots. Don't know anything.' When she does not respond, he follows her into the bathroom. 'And of all the fucking idiots, the fuckingest of all is Frank Rosen.' He gives a little grin and repeats it. 'Fuckingest of all. Hasn't a clue.'

Previously, she would have encouraged him to get undressed, given him some Disprin and some Prohep and put him to bed.

'I hate Frank, d'you know that, Maria? Frank is . . . Frank is the devil.'

He follows her back into the bedroom, stands behind her as she throws her shoes into the wardrobe, unclips her necklace and removes her earrings.

'I need a break, you know, Maria. I need to get away.' He follows her back into the bathroom. As she starts to unbutton her blouse, she is suddenly aware of wanting to shield her nakedness from him.

'Get out, Jake. I need to bath.'

He flops on to the bed. Within seconds he is snoring. When he wakes she will be gone.

TWENTY-THREE

IT IS THE last week of term. And yet, instead of winding down, the exhibition seems to have stirred his students up. They have many questions: Why do some paintings sell and not others? Is it the luck of the draw? To what extent should you cater for your 'market'? Zara does not bother to attend. Infuriating girl. This time he's not running after her. Besides, he has more important things to think about: Maria has left home. He can't decide what to do about it. Bloody inconvenient, her timing, that's all he can say. And unbelievably inconsiderate. Trudy has mentioned that Frank Rosen had called to find out Zara's address. Apparently, he wants to see more paintings. Idiot. The man is unspeakably narrow-minded. They should get on well together, Frank and Zara, he muses acidly. Both are dirty and have no manners.

A car grinds to a halt on the gravel outside. She hears a man's heavy tread, and then the knock on the door. Laika sniffs under the door and barks. She opens the door as far as the security latch will allow. An unshaven man is standing on the stoep holding a cigarette and a business card.

'Are you Zara Pascal?' he asks. 'Frank Rosen,' he

adds, before she has time to nod. He hands her the business card. 'May I come in?'

He walks around the tiny room, looking at the etchings, the drawings and paintings either hanging on the wall, or stacked against it.

'I bought your painting the other night,' he says, walking across to the window to flick the ash from his cigarette. 'Do you have more?'

She does not respond. He does not seem to mind.

'Yours was the only one worth buying. Thought I'd find out what else you had.'

She sits down, the dog guarding her feet, while he rummages among the paintings.

'Oh, I hope you don't mind if I look at these?' he asks after a while, not waiting for a reply. 'Is this your best work?'

'I don't know,' she says.

'Do you have anything else?'

'I have a portfolio of paintings. They're at the school.'

'Coleman's school?'

'Yes.'

'God. Why?'

Again, she does not answer.

'No, seriously,' he probes. 'What made you go to his school? What can he teach you?'

'My grandfather thought I should go. He thought it would be good for me.'

'And you?'

'I don't mind. I like it sometimes.'

'What if I told you that you don't need art school? At least, not that one.'

She shrugs.

'What if I told you that I'm pretty sure you can earn a living without them?'

Again she does not respond.

'Naturally nothing is certain. But I reckon I could get you an income of sorts, if you were prepared to paint full-time.'

She shrugs and looks out of the window. 'That would be good.'

'Think about it,' he says.

He gets the class going with informal discussion. A post-exhibition forum for feedback and questions. So far these have been lively with some probing issues raised.

One of the quieter students puts up her hand. 'What if we are inspired by the style of another painter, say Kentridge for example? Is it okay to copy some of the elements from his work, to borrow aspects of style from other painters?'

'Well,' he says with a smile, 'you must know what Picasso says about that: Small artists borrow. Great artists steal.'

A scruffy youth – one of considerable talent – shakes his head slowly, as though shaking ideas from the dreadlocks, and answers: 'I dunno. I don't think that's, like, too cool, to use too much of other painters' stuff. It should, like, come from yourself, don't you think?'

'Maybe it can be, like, a bit of both? I dunno,' says another.

They all look questioningly at him. Trusting him, the oracle, to give them the correct answer.

He begins slowly. 'I think it's both and . . .'

They wait expectantly for him to explain. He pauses, thinking. 'In some ways, we are the sum total of all that has moved us, affected us and touched us. The sum total of all of our experiences.'

Some of them nod.

'And whether we are painters or writers or poets – artists of any kind, we are collectors and creators, of, of *meaning*. If you'll pardon the cliché.'

'And of beauty,' the quiet girl adds.

'Sure. But that lends itself to another conversation. Let's stick with copying other artists' work. It's not that simple, you see. I believe that every painter, whether consciously or subconsciously, is born into a tradition. Many are shaped by a particular style or movement, even if only to rebel against it later. It provides a framework within which to comply or rebel. It defines you by its presence or its reaction away from it. Cubism, for instance, is both a reaction against and a development from Impressionism. But as for blind copying, that is something else. That is ultimately betraying yourself. By all means, allow a work, or a canon of work, to affect you on different levels. But make sure it is integrated into your entire being. Only when it becomes part of your substance, your flesh, absorbed into your bone marrow, your *blood,* are you free to use it responsibly. Because you will be painting from *your* core, not from someone else's. From the atom-splitting centre of your *own* consciousness. Anything else is simply cutting and pasting. Window dressing. Re-packaging and selling. A magpie collage of other people's inspiration.' He tries to swallow the nausea his own loquacity stirs up in his guts.

The class disperse and settle at their easels. He sits down. He knows that somewhere over the last few years, as long as a decade even, he has stopped practising what he has just preached. He has borrowed and adapted and painted what *works*. Decoration. Pleasing pieces for those with a wealth of money but a poverty of substance. Perpetuating the 'con' in contemporary art. Riding the gravy train to its life-clogging destination.

The realisation is both damning and liberating. The immediate implications branch and split off like lightning; again the nausea stirs inside him, stronger this time. He is a fake. And not only is he a fake, but he has somehow, miraculously, managed to build a reputation on it! The old demons lift their heads and rub their eyes, getting ready for the dance. The mad dance of panic. He feels his chest tighten. Catches his breath. It's coming. It's coming again.

'Excuse me,' he says. 'Excuse me, I'm not feeling well.'

He walks as quickly as he can to his office.

'Jake!' Trudy has been waiting for him. Follows him down the corridor.'

'Leave me alone,' he snarls. He is not up to interrogation.

'Wait! I need to talk to you.'

'Leave me alone, goddammit! Are you deaf?'

She shrinks back, too shocked to know how to react. Too horrified to find an immediate excuse for him. 'Okay,' she whispers as his office door slams, deciding that she'll give him a few minutes, then go and see whether she can help.

He slumps on to the chair. His heart is tearing away inside his chest. This time. This time surely he is going to die. And he will die a fake. A life wasted. His meagre talent prostituted. And nobody to blame but himself. The handle of his door turns.

Zara.

'Don't you ever bloody knock?' he growls.

She stands there looking at him. Suddenly her blank gaze seems insolent. Mocking.

'What's the matter with you? Who do you think you are? You never knock. You never answer when you're spoken to.'

'I have left some paintings here,' she says. 'My portfolio. I need to pick it up.'

'What are you talking about?'

'Frank Rosen came to see me. He wants to see more paintings.'

He feels the blood rise thick in his throat. It's true, what they say about love and hate. It really *is* the same thing!

'Zara, please,' he tries to gather himself. 'Look, please go away. I'm not feeling well. Okay?' He attempts a smile.

But she ignores him, moving across the room to his desk, where her portfolio lies. Before she can get past him he takes hold of her, turns her around, seizes her hair in his hand and holds her upturned face in a firm grip. He does not hear the soft knocking at the door. With his other hand he squeezes her mouth, before parting her lips with his fingers and possessing her mouth with his own. She gives a little cry.

'Am I hurting you?' he murmurs.

'Yes.'

'Good.'

He stops and looks at her. Perhaps if he cannot elicit love, he can at least provoke fear. But her eyes are shut. He will never know. He releases her. Just in time to see Trudy close the door again. He can hear her heels clicking down the corridor as she runs away.

'Get out,' he hisses. 'Now! Get out.'

But she does not leave. She simply stands there looking him directly in the eye. She is mocking him. He feels sure of it. She probably knows. Knows he's a fake. That is why she has no respect for him at all.

'I'm not coming back next term,' she says evenly. 'I am going to have to paint from home. I need the money. I wanted to tell you.'

How dare she! Nobody, not a single soul has ever, *ever*, attended his school and found it wanting. As she lifts her hand to touch his face (sympathy? derision?), he catches it and throws it down, before taking her by the shoulders, forcibly, to turn her round and push her in the direction of the door.

In weeks to come, when he runs it through his mind time and again, he will still not fathom exactly what happened at this point. He pushed her firmly, he will concede. But not roughly. Not forcefully enough for her to fall. She is not a small girl. All he can think is that she refused to budge, refused to move her feet, and the push knocked her off balance. Much later, he wonders if she didn't perhaps faint?

To see Zara collapsed on the floor, powerless, seems bizarre. If he didn't know better, he would think she was looking for attention. She lies huddled awkwardly, unmoving, her skirt hitched up. Her face does not move. She says nothing. As he stares at her, nonplussed, he notices a line of blood spreading into a small puddle beneath her.

'Zara.' He drops to his knees.

But she does not answer.

'Zara.' She doesn't hear.

'It was a tiny push. I couldn't have hurt you. It was just a tiny push. Are you sick?'

When again she doesn't answer, he grabs his car keys and, scooping her up in his arms, manoeuvres her out of the door, kicking it shut with his foot. Then along the passage, down the stairs, to the car, to the hospital.

He carries her into the hospital through the automatic doors. His breath is getting shorter and faster. He feels light-headed. Suddenly she raises her head.

'Stop,' she says.

'What?'

'Stop. Let me walk. Put me down.'

He lowers her legs to the ground.

'I'm okay,' she says.

'You were bleeding, Zara. Please. For once in your life don't be so bloody stubborn. We must get you checked.'

He sits in the waiting room while Zara is being examined by a doctor from the emergency ward. Remembers the Valium in his wallet and asks a nurse for a glass of water. He cannot think all this through now. One step at a time. Just one step at a time is all he need worry about. After some time the doctor reappears and calls Jake into his office. Zara is sitting quietly in a chair. Serene.

'Is she okay?'

'She is probably going to lose her baby. She tells me she was not aware that she is pregnant.'

'What?'

'Is this your wife? Your girlfriend? Mr . . .?'

'Coleman. Doctor. Dr Jake Coleman.'

'The painter? Look, it's none of my business what your relationship is. But I suggest you go away and discuss whether you want this baby or not. If not, you're welcome to come back here, or leave her here overnight. The gynaecologist, Mr Le Roux, should be able to help her in the morning.'

'Patrick Le Roux?'

'Yes. Do you know him?'

'Er, no. Heard of him. Look, I'd rather not wait until then, she was bleeding, there may be a problem. Is there any other gynaecologist perhaps? Someone who could help her now? Besides, tomorrow is awkward for me. Impossible, in fact.'

'The bleeding has stopped. It is quite possible that she could go full term without any further complications.'

'I'd rather not take the chance,' says Jake. 'It's out of the question. It must be removed.'

'What about you?' The doctor turns to Zara.

She stares back at him without a sound. Shrugs.

'Well, there are clinics that are . . . functional. It may be your best bet if discretion is an issue.'

'Clinics?'

'They do terminations. It's a similar procedure. Quite above board. Done by a gynaecologist. It's cheaper too, of course. Personally, I would prefer her to stay here, but she's not very far gone. It should be okay.'

'That sounds better. The clinic. Do you have an address?'

She walks with him down a busy street. He is still holding the piece of paper in his hand with the address, looking up at the names of the side streets till he finds the right one. She follows him. Past the big clothing stores, the shops selling African artwork and a fish shop that has 'wind-dried snoek' written on a blackboard outside the door. She has not said a word since they left the hospital. She is unusually meek, he thinks. Perhaps she is in shock.

'It is for the best,' he tells her.

She is silent.

'You must agree, Zara?'

But she is absent. As though her mind has finally vacated her body. All the more reason to go through with it, he reassures himself with a little nod.

Trucks block the traffic, cars hoot, hawkers shout, people walk with purpose, crossing the road, looking right to left.

The sun is bright and cheery. Just like any other day. The door to the Elizabeth Scott Clinic just like any other door. But then, what did he expect? A big X marked in ox-blood? He stops at the door. Crams a wad of money into her hand, before awkwardly moving away.

'I'll be back later.' He tries to smile. 'Good luck.'

She walks into the room. There are Aids posters on the walls. Carpet tiles. Plastic orange bucket chairs. The receptionist gives a cheery grin and hands her a form. Everything seems surreal. Muddled. Once she has completed it, the woman smiles, takes a happy slurp of her coffee and beckons. 'Come on then, let me give you your gown.'

She changes into the white polycotton nightgown with small purple flowers, removes her panties as instructed, and is led into a room with several other women, heads cast down, all dressed in the same faded fabric. Somehow the outfit seems bizarre, too pretty, too fresh. The air conditioning hums and outside people are innocently going about the business of the day. Such an ordinary day to do such a thing.

The waiting is eternal. A squat girl who sits with her legs apart starts to giggle raucously. Nerves. The rest look down. A pretty girl with long brown hair wiggles her painted toes. A large fat redhead sits traumatised, her head in her hands. Still the air conditioning hums and a Coloured man outside shouts something to a friend across the street.

Eventually, a tall, big-boned nurse opens the door and calls her name. Zara follows her meekly down the passage into a cramped room. She tries to think of something peaceful. But everything is confused. She keeps forgetting why she is here. Strange pictures are forming in her mind.

She is playing by the waterfall with Laika. It is a Saturday and Blom and Pieter are at home with their families. Pappi has gone to Cape Town to get some provisions although everybody knows that Saturday is a horses day, that he is off to bet on number thirteen, and nobody asks questions. She and Laika are swimming and rescuing bugs. She fishes out a beautiful red beetle, and puts it on a leaf in the sun. Then they lie down in the warm mud and watch the bright male weavers deftly threading their hanging house baskets before their disapproving mates arrive and pull them all down. In time the wind picks up and it grows cold. 'Come, Laika, let's go back and get a jersey.'

In the room at the end of the passage at the clinic, there is a bed with stirrups attached with clamps. And a fat and freckled man squashing a long lock of ginger hair down over his ruddy, bald patch. 'C'mon, luvvie,' he says a little too cheerily. 'Jump up then, there's a good girl.' In his hand is something glinting silver. 'C'mon now.' He pats the bed.

Zara lies on the bed. 'Feet in the stirrups then, there you go,' he says. But she does not hear him. 'C'mon luv, we don't have all day, let's get the show on the road, shall we? Feet in the stirrups.' *Saturday is horses day.* When she does not respond, he gives a big sigh, and squashes the errant lock of ginger hair over his bald patch once again.

'It's easier with stirrups, luv. Come on then, play the game.'

He asks the nurse to help him. While forcing her knees apart, the two make congenial noises, as though she is six years old. As though they are encouraging her to ride a bicycle for the first time without fairy wheels.

She reaches up and with both hands pushes open the front door. 'Maman?' There is a funny smell. Sour. Laika drops down, his belly scuffing the floor. He begins to growl. Something is happening in the bedroom. Muffled noises. 'Maman?'

She rounds the door of the bedroom to find Maman lying on the bed, her clothes ripped. Blood. A man stands over her, his trousers by his ankles, a knife glinting in one hand, his other hand over Maman's mouth. Whether it is because Laika starts barking and snarling and snapping at the man, or because seeing her child suddenly gives her superhuman strength, who can say? But at that moment Maman only just manages to raise her knees and kick her attacker away with sufficient force to free her mouth and scream:

'Leave my baby, for God's sake leave my baby!'

Lying on the bed, Zara can see the shiny implement the gynaecologist is holding out of the corner of her eye, as sharp and clear as the memory that is gathering momentum inside her. *The knife. Her mother. Blood.* As he tries to insert it into her, from the depths of her silence rips a primeval scream. And as she screams she too kicks with the full force of her being, with both feet, knocking him into the wall.

'No! I don't want you to! I say *no*. Leave my baby!'

*

Maddened further by pain, the intruder lunges at Maman with the knife. Only time enough for her to shout: 'Run, Zara. Run!' before he starts stabbing her repeatedly in the head and chest. When he turns to Zara, she has fled. A blood-flecked speck, running as fast as she can into the mountains.

It is Pieter who finds her the following day, lost in the mountains, wide-eyed, huddled by some rocks. It is Laika who shows him where she is. Laika who has followed her every step of the way, and who barks and barks till someone hears. It is Pieter who watches her being driven away by Dr Belotti to the big hospital in Cape Town, where she is treated for shock. Pieter already knows that Camille is dead. Everybody in the valley is talking about it, phoning one another and shaking their heads as though she had been their friend. As though they cared. When Pieter rides across to find Zara, there are policemen wanting to ask questions, but Pappi sends them away. There is no point anyway. Zara does not remember a thing.

When Pieter returns the following day, the policemen are back again in yellow vans. Taking fingerprints. Trying to pick up clues. Talking to Pappi. He feels scared. Hides behind the big oak tree.

'Are you sure your granddaughter doesn't remember anything?' he hears them ask.

'Quite sure,' Pappi answers.

'Have you asked her recently?'

'Listen, you idiot, I'm her grandfather. I know. Have a look at that face for yourself. Have a look at those eyes. They are the emptied-out eyes of the living dead. There is no memory there. Nothing. Now leave us alone.'

But they ignore Pappi and keep pressing on. He

wishes they would listen. He wishes they would go away. But most of all he wishes that Camille would appear in the doorway, call him in for some juice and Zoo biscuits, press the indent between his eyebrows and tell him not to worry. That everything would be fine.

'Are you sure you have no clue who may have done this, Mr Pascal? There are a lot of natives around lately. They're a savage bunch. Have any been hanging around here?'

Pappi tries not to lose his patience.

'The people who came to the clinic were ill. They came because they needed help, not because they wanted to rape and murder my daughter.'

'But maybe they were just pretending to be ill. They wanted to check things out, you know? They do that.'

'You know, Inspector, I have not lived here that long. But this much I do know: in this country it could have been anybody. Nobody of any colour, shape or creed seems to escape the dry brain rot here. A psychopath would be quite comfortable in any environment you choose. Yes, it could have been one of the labourers, blind drunk and violent after a night's drinking. Or one of the black people, erupting out of the mire of repression. Or the witch doctor, angry with her for interfering with his power. Or one of you! It could even have been one of you, the white people of this place. After all, nobody seems to sin quite as expertly as you Calvinists. Pah!' He spits on the ground next to them.

'I see,' says the inspector. After that, they do not return.

'The patient is still very upset,' the receptionist at the clinic tells Jake when he returns.

'That's understandable, I suppose.' Jake knows he should not have returned. This is sordid. He does not belong here.

'We're going to keep her here for a few hours, till she stabilises. Are you her boyfriend?'

'Boyfriend? No.' What a ridiculous term.

'Friend? Father?'

He pauses to think. It is a good question. 'Actually, I hardly know her,' he finally answers.

'Does she have any relatives?'

'I don't know,' says Jake, edging towards the door. It is not his place to get involved in the details. 'I don't know. Really, if I have to be honest, I hardly know her at all.' Then he escapes into the street outside and closes the door behind him.

The gynaecologist from the clinic is undamaged by Zara's kick. He is, however, convinced that the patient needs some time to reconsider her decision to terminate the pregnancy.

'She may have been pushed into it; you know how it goes. She seems to be in a bit of shock. Will somebody please make her some tea.'

She does not drink the tea. She is not feeling very well, she says. After a while, she asks the nurse whether she may use the telephone.

'Feeling queasy?' the nurse tries to make conversation after she puts the receiver down. 'S'normal.'

Zara stares out of the window.

'Aaai, you look so sad.' The nurse walks across and pats her hand. 'It's gonna be okay, you know. In the end it's always okay.'

'My mother died,' says Zara evenly, turning to face the nurse. 'She was murdered. It will never be okay.'

*

'A young man came to pick her up,' the nurse later tells the gynaecologist. 'Just double-parked his Mazda outside and came running inside. He looked okay. Much better than the one who brought her in.' She shakes her head. 'Something in that face of hers. I don't know, Doctor. Terrible pain. I'm just glad she left with that boy. Did you see her eyes?'

TWENTY-FOUR

Icy wind drives rain like little shards of glass into the heart and soul of both city and country. The Cape winter seems to have arrived overnight. People in raincoats scurry, shoulders hunched, under soaking umbrellas, held at forty-five-degree angles as they dash from their cars to the shop, anxious to get the day's chores done so that they can return to dry homes and log fires. The gallery has been quiet for days. Maria sits, elbows on the counter, and takes a long drag from her cigarette. Smoke curls upward. Still no news from Jake. The strain of waiting for his voice at the other end of the line increases hourly, and as the implications set in, pain turns to fear. He might never phone again. Then what? She cannot sleep at night, and when she does, it is the sleep of the sick, pocked with dreams. The same dreams. Dreams of being lost in a deserted town on a desolate Sunday afternoon, driving the wrong way up one-way streets, calling, searching, hearing only echoes. And the anger. *The anger*. Acid in her chest. How Jake has rustled with secrets all these years. The master of discretion. Which may or may not be the better part of valour, but certainly is also the convenient little brother of deceit.

And yet all her events and achievements seem such a hollow celebration without him. And the future so long and dry.

She ended up going for that tarot reading advertised in *Odyssey* magazine. She hoped it might clarify things. The woman reading the cards was getting on in years. She had papery white skin and very black hair. And an exaggerated air of knowing. She sliced and diced the cards, swooshed them across the table and had Maria pick and choose. She began with three cards, to indicate past, present and future. Then went on to do a six-month forecast. But all Maria can really remember are two cards: the hanged man and the devil card. The Hanged Man, when appearing the right way up, the woman explained, meant that everything is not as it seems on the surface. She gave Maria a long knowing look. And then produced the Devil Card. This, she said slowly, while nodding her head and narrowing her eyes, indicated wilful blindness and misconception. A willingness to be bound by half-truths. Maria couldn't wait to leave. Nothing new. So why can't she just cut her losses – God knows there are many – and move on? She needs to do something completely different. Perhaps she should get away. Take a good long break, and reassess her life. Ten years she has poured into making his life a success. She almost doesn't know how to do the same for herself. What she needs is a big idea. If only she could think of one.

But love is a tough habit to break.

At least she has a safe place to stay. Mátyás's house may not be the largest, nor the cleanest. But it is welcoming and warm. And safe.

'You stay here as long as you need to,' he insisted when she called him the day she moved out. 'It's a treat for me to have company.'

She decides to close the shop early. She knows Mátyás will have a fire going, and nobody is coming into the gallery on a day like today. In the rain, the trip to Glencairn is a little treacherous in parts, roads glassy, traffic backed up here and there. But inside the plush interior of her car she feels cocooned, the rhythm of the windscreen wipers comfortingly hypnotic.

By the time she reaches the small, wooden A-frame, she is nursing a strong sense of relief. Mátyás stands at the door. She catches the pungent aroma of coffee.

'I've just made coffee. Would you like some?'

She sits on the bench at the rough wooden table, while he fills two pottery mugs with the dark brew.

'Aren't you ever lonely here, Mátyás?'

'I've grown used to it, I suppose. You can be more lonely surrounded by people you don't care for, and who don't care for you.'

'Do you think so?'

'Yes. Anyway, I am not alone. I have you to keep me company for now. And when it is not you, I have my memories.'

'A woman?' she probes.

'Isn't it always?'

'Was she beautiful?'

'They often are, the ones you love. And if love doesn't make them beautiful, then memory will always do so.'

'I don't know,' she says. She knows only too well that Jake does not think her beautiful. Not any more. 'Tell me about her.'

'Oh, it was a long, long time ago. You don't want to hear my little story.'

'Oh, but I do. At this moment, there is nothing I would like more. Please, tell me.'

'Yes?' He looks a little embarrassed.

'Yes,' she nods with enthusiasm.

'Well, let's see. It all started with a broken leg, about

twenty years ago. I was in France for a friend's exhibition. One lunchtime, I had too much red wine, and next thing, *Poef!* I came off my *vélocette* in the rain. It wasn't very bad, but due to the nature of the break I had to lie still, in traction, for some weeks. Naturally I had books, magazines, even a sketchpad, but I couldn't really sit up long enough to draw. So for most of the day, and long stretches of the night, I was very bored. I would sing. The man in the bed opposite said I had a voice like a badly oiled steam locomotive. But I didn't care. Anything to break the predictable patterns and routines. The nurses would tell me to *tais-toi!* To shut up. But I didn't care. They were bossy little women. Except for one.' His dark eyes twinkle. 'She was a night nurse. Came on at seven. She was different from the other nurses; soft and soothing like the sound of water. I would wait for her all day, just to watch her move across the floor. Even in her thick, starched white uniform she was very sexy. She worked very hard and took no nonsense when we tried to flirt with her, but now and again she would catch my eye and smile in a way that encouraged me to believe that it was not only I who felt this way.

'One night I asked her whether she would bring me a writing pad so that I could write letters during the day. The next day she handed me a folder of fine onion-skin paper and some envelopes. Beautiful. And then I started writing. Every day I wrote a letter. I wrote of all the little things I could think of that had ever made me happy or sad. Every day I would try to remember a new one. About the village where I grew up in Hungary. About sitting in the basket of my father's bicycle. About my fear of the dark. I started to remember more and more, and the more I wrote the more came back to me. How bad my first kiss was. How the girl had run off laughing at me and told all her friends! The first time I saw the sea.

'Of course, she could not know at first, but the letters were for her. I told her almost everything, and especially all my "first times". My first hiding, my first fight, the first time I felt jealous, and even the first time I made love. Because, you see, every night I saw her was like reliving the thrill of all the first times I had ever had. It was like seeing in colour all over again. Just watching her walk across the ward and waiting for that quick wingflap of recognition.

'In time, I did let her know that the letters were for her. She would come for them only once she was sure I was asleep. I never saw her reading them, and she never stayed to talk. She gave no feedback at all. Very professional. But the night before I was due to be discharged, it was she who left an envelope in the folder.'

'A letter?'

'Yes. A long letter of just these two words: *I know*. And her address.' He laughs. 'After that we were together every afternoon and weekend for three weeks. She was still working the nightshift; I don't know when she slept.' He shakes his head. 'And then of course, I had to go back to Hungary. I told her I'd be back.' He picks up the coffee pot, refills Maria's mug and sighs.

'You never came back?'

'I came back.' She picks up the edges of defensiveness in his voice. 'But it was too late, she had gone.'

'Too late? How long were you?'

'A year. I had some trouble. I sent a letter. But she didn't wait.'

'I don't understand.'

He pauses. Adjusts his big frame awkwardly on the wooden bench. 'I was married at the time.'

'Ah.' Maria's eyes widen. She takes a slug of coffee. 'I suppose that can do it.'

'Separated from my wife for some time when I met her. But Dorci – my wife – and I had almost grown up together. And when I returned to finalise the divorce, we discovered she was ill. Lymphoma.' He sighs. 'So I had to write and tell my night nurse.'

'In hospital, all those letters you wrote and left in the folder each night for her, you never told her you were married?'

'No.'

'So how did you come to South Africa? To Glencairn, of all places.'

'I learned she had come to South Africa. I wanted to follow.'

'How did you know? Did she write?'

'Not to me.'

'Then?'

'Well, after my wife died, I returned to France. It was only then that I discovered she had left, seemingly without trace. She could be quite highly strung. I didn't know her very long, but I sensed she could be a little impulsive. And spontaneous, which was lovely. Anyway, the neighbours didn't seem to know. The hospital told me they were not prepared to disclose private information. Eventually, after pleading with several different members and levels of staff, I left my address with one of the other nurses and returned to Hungary. Some years later I received a letter from this nurse, to tell me that she had died in South Africa, in the Cape, and that was all she knew.'

'God. And you still came?'

'Yes. Just because a relationship stops, doesn't mean it ends. Besides, my wife had died. She had died. It was

234

winter and icy in Hungary, and frankly I was tired of it. I wanted to live somewhere in the sun. It was either here or Spain. So I gave up my studio apartment, actually I gave up painting altogether, and moved here. Somehow that brought me closer to believing I was still keeping my word. Who knows, maybe I hoped to meet her ghost. Maybe I hoped to find my bearings.' He leans forward and smiles. 'Do you know that one of the thirteenth-century interpretations of the word "desire" comes from the Latin *de sidos*, which means to have lost one's navigational star?'

'You gave up *painting*? I never knew you painted.'

'Yes. After all that it was just too painful. Pottery, clay, was, is, so wonderfully earthy. It grounds one so.'

'Do you have any paintings? Anything I could see?' Already her eyes are sweeping across the walls, looking for a clue, a relic. But there is nothing. Mátyás studies the empty mug, as though reading the lees, moves his heavy body on the bench and finally shakes his head.

'No, not really. Just the painting in the bedroom.'

'That's *yours*? I noticed that last time. Very powerful.'

They lapse into silence. Eventually, it is Maria who looks up, reaches across the table and takes his hand.

'Thanks for telling me that. It couldn't have been easy. You helped take my mind off things.'

'You are the first one I've ever told. I should thank you.'

'I'm sure you don't have to tell anybody to keep a memory like that alive.'

'Yes, memories are easy. It is forgetting one must learn!' He laughs. 'But listen to me. I'm getting maudlin. Can we blame the coffee? Do we need some wine? Let's have some food, yes?'

'But Mátyás, aren't you ever angry? Don't you think she should have waited, if she really loved you? Don't you think she should have tried to understand a little?'

'Memories, like dreams, are funny things. They don't stand too much poking.'

He fetches two plates from the dresser and dishes up for her. 'Some pasta and salad?'

'It smells wonderful. What is it?'

'Aubergine and olives and nuts.'

'This is the first time in a while I've felt like eating.'

'Your heart is sore. When the heart is sore, the stomach closes shop.'

She blinks and tries to smile.

'Don't be so brave,' he says. 'It's okay if you cry. I won't run out of the door into the rain.'

She digs into her food. He watches her before he begins himself.

'You need something to look forward to, Maria. A plan, just for you.'

'It sounds lonely.'

'It doesn't have to be. It can be a plan that includes many people. I'm sure if you think about it, and allow yourself to think big, the right one will come, yes?'

'I keep thinking I should go away, but I really don't know where to go.'

'You're not listening well enough,' he says. 'But you need silence in your mind before you can hear.'

'There is always so much noise,' she says. 'Everywhere I go, there seem to be people banging and building, or playing blaring music. So much noise.' The tears are sticking in her throat. 'I must blow my nose,' she smiles weakly.

As she walks through the room with the roughly

made bed, she stops to look at the enormous painting hanging above the bed. A painting of a woman. Intriguing face.

When she returns he is deep in thought.

'You know, it's a funny thing. Like I said, nobody knows this story, except you. But the other night, at your exhibition . . .'

'You mean *that* exhibition,' she smiles ruefully.

'Yes, *that* one.' He grins, then frowns. 'There was a painting . . .'

'Pascal.'

'How did you know?'

'It was the best piece by far. Anybody who knew anything could see that. Even Jake. And Frank Rosen actually bought it! He's never done that before.'

'It disturbed me,' he says slowly.

'It was an extremely disturbing work.'

'No, that's not why.'

'No?'

'No. The girl's face. I don't know.'

'Did it remind you? Of this woman?'

'There was something. And then when I saw it was the same surname, I was thrown a little.'

'Pascal?'

'Yes.'

'Was that her last name, this woman?'

'Yes. Pascal, Camille Pascal.'

'So, are you going to do anything about it? Find out more?'

'I don't know. Like I say, sometimes memories don't stand too much poking.'

As she climbs under the rough covers that night, staring

at the sloping wooden ceiling above her, Mátyás's words come back to her: *You need something to look forward to, Maria. A plan, just for you.* The devil tarot card suggested that the bonds that tie her are of her own volition. If she could only think of an idea big enough to propel her through her own self-doubts and beyond. *Think big, Maria. Think big.*

TWENTY-FIVE

JAKE RETURNS TO the school a day before term begins again. He looks up at the building as though he were seeing it again for the first time after a very long journey away. The big white gables, the polished red stoep, the big teak door, the coffee table with the imported art magazines, the corridors, the staircase. He knows every corner; it has the familiarity of an old lover. He climbs the stairs to his office, unlocks the door and looks around. Everything as it was. Everything disarmingly the same. This is his world. His reality. His kingdom. This is where he belongs, in the realms of beauty and learning. Everything else, everything that has happened in the last few weeks, has been a dream. A bad dream. He hopes he can forget about it soon. He notices a crisp white envelope on the floor. Someone must have pushed it under the door. He picks it up then sits at his desk. While he waits for his computer to boot up, he slits open the letter.

Dear Jake,
   I wish to tender my resignation with immediate effect.
Yours faithfully,
Trudy

He sighs. Nods. It is time. In fact, it is a little overdue. So much of a relationship is knowing when to leave. And she left it a little late, he feels. In fact, come to think of it, just as people tend to be remembered by their last job, 90 per cent of a memory is in the ending. Is that not what dictates whether one remembers or *dismembers* time spent together? He feels a wave of pity. Poor little kitten. All her illusions bitten open by light. It is never an easy lesson to learn that light has teeth. Ah, where, where does it go, the love when it has died? Is that a song? He digs in his drawer for a business card for an employment agency he has always found helpful.

'Yes of course, we'd love to help, Dr Coleman. We can send some candidates over very soon. Maybe even later this morning.'

In his e-mail inbox, there is a note from the Dutch gallery owners who had been out to see him. They had returned to Holland after a good trip, they said. Sorry that they missed him. And would he be interested in being part of an exhibition in Amsterdam in three months' time?

His reply is short.

Dear Sirs,
Thank you for thinking of me for your exhibition. It would have been an honour to accept your invitation. However, I have decided to take an extended sabbatical from painting to recharge the batteries and nourish the soul. In the meantime, I will be concentrating on building the international profile of my art school. I wish you everything of the best in your venture.
Yours truly,
Jake Coleman (Dr)

What relief. The decision had come to him overnight after weeks of mind-mangling wrestling. He would take a break. God knows he deserves one after all he's been through. And then Maria would help him relaunch his career when he was ready.

Maria. He wants Maria, he has decided. Capable, dependable Maria. He has really missed her these last few weeks. Especially in the early hours of the morning. When he woke this morning, the thought suddenly struck him that she might never return. Usually she would have contacted him by now.

He called her immediately.

'Can I come and have coffee with you this afternoon?' he asked in a small voice.

There was the slightest of pauses.

'Okay.' Maria is usually so welcoming, but there was a new briskness to her tone. Defensive. But she agreed. The rest should be easy.

He watches her walk towards him. She has lost a considerable amount of weight, yet still has 'body'. In fact, she looks rather appealing. He expected her to fall to pieces without him; in some ways he feels a little offended that she hasn't. But then, Maria is a remarkable woman. She has always had her own identity. And a thirst for living that nobody could quench. How could he have forgotten that? He smiles. How attractive she appears. Is there anything in the world as desirable as a woman who is only just out of reach, even if sometimes he has to put her there himself? It only confirms what he has always thought: the eternal illusory quest for the perfect mirror can only be sustained from a distance. He slowly stirs a spoon of brown sugar into his cappuccino, watching her all the while.

'I've missed you,' he says.

'Why?' she says.

'Because I love you.'

'Please. You don't honestly expect me to believe that.'

'No, I don't expect anything. But at least allow me my self-recriminations.'

She stares at him for a while, exhaling a stream of cigarette smoke to one side.

'Don't make me grovel, Maria.'

'For what? What do you want, Jake?'

He looks at her. She can sense him retract. The scales revert. He pushes his cappuccino away. Makes as if to stand up.

'Okay. This was a bad idea. I always thought you a generous woman, Maria. A kind and tolerant woman. Big-hearted. Clearly I was wrong. When are you coming to get the rest of your things?'

'Jake, wait. Please. You must see it's not easy for me. How do you expect me to feel? For months, maybe years, I don't know, you've been screwing your secretary. Do you honestly just expect me to put up with that?'

'I haven't been screwing my secretary. And in any case, she's leaving.'

'Jake, I saw you. At the exhibition, by the car. You can't deny it. You're lying!'

'I'm not lying.' He looks outraged.

'No, of course not. You never lie, Jake. How could I forget that. You simply edit the truth.'

'I don't believe you!' he snaps backs. 'After knowing me for ten years you choose to make up some paranoid story just because you see me comforting someone. That's all I was doing. Comforting her. And for that you kick up all this fuss? And all this right now, when I needed you the most. Does the word "integrity" mean anything to you at all, Maria?' He makes as if to leave again.

'Wait, Jake! Let's finish this conversation.' Her voice is pleading.

Then suddenly she sees it: she's *fallen* for it. Again! The fear of him leaving has always been larger than anything. Larger than herself. And nobody knows it better than he. That he who can walk away the easiest calls the shots.

Mátyás's words return to her yet again: *You need something to look forward to, Maria. A plan, just for you.*

She lifts her large suede handbag from the floor and puts it on her lap.

'She's leaving?' she repeats more calmly. She feels inside the handbag slowly, taking care that he does not notice. Touches the signed sale papers for the gallery. They are still there. A totem.

'Yes. I decided if she were upsetting you that much, she must go. But clearly I'm more committed to this relationship than you are. This is the thanks I get.'

She slides her hand further into the bag till she feels a smoother surface. The Cunard brochure with her single round-the-world ticket on the *QE2* already inside.

'Have you found a replacement?' she asks lightly. Her fingertips glide over the glossy brochure cover like a secret caress. Just a few more days before she flies to Spain to catch up with the ship. It will be warmer there. She'll get a suntan.

'The employment agency sent a girl across this morning.'

'Any good?'

243

As he drains the liquid from the avant-garde mug he thinks of the young lady he interviewed that morning. Raven-haired with a perfect little widow's peak, accentuating her already heart-shaped face. A full, sensuous mouth that smiled every time he spoke to her. Eager to please. She asked for his autograph.

'Yes,' he says, wiping his mouth with the serviette. 'I think she will do perfectly.'

ACKNOWLEDGEMENTS

The quotation on the page preceding Part 1 is from the poem 'The Hooded Hawk' by Anne Michaels in *Skin Divers* published by Bloomsbury. The metaphor 'guests of this earth' on p. 130 is inspired by her poem 'Ice House', in the same volume.

Jake's research for his Rodin lecture in Chapter 11 is drawn from the essay 'Myths of Creation: Camille Claudel & Auguste Rodin' by Anne Higonnet, from the book *Significant Others*, edited by Whitney Chadwick and Isabelle de Courtivron.

Many people were instrumental in the writing of this book, some directly, some indirectly: I would like to thank André, and Geoff, without whose unflagging support, encouragement and friendship, the lines on these pages would still be voiceless.

Glen, trusted critic and life-friend, for that winter, listening.

I am also deeply grateful to those who believed, often without me – my parents, Niall and Carol. And, of course, Sue, Lisa, Alta'tjie, Sherrill, Cherie, Dorian, Roger, and Bernie.

The Mendelssohns, all of them, past and present, here and there. And especially Donna, who long ago got me to say 'I am a writer' to myself until it became more than a whisper.

Riccardo, for many reasons, but mostly just for being Riccardo.

And finally, Marleen, the fairy, who really did teach me how to fly.

To all of you. This book is yours too. I hold you in my heart, my hands. Thank you.